This book should be returned to any branch of the
Lancashire County Library on or before the date shown

2 5 JUN 2015

SUT
SCG

Lancashire County Library
Bowran Street
Preston PR1 2UX
www.lancashire.gov.uk/libraries

Also by Clive Goddard

Fintan Fedora
the World's Worst Explorer

FINTAN FEDORA
EXPLORES AGAIN

CLIVE GODDARD

SCHOLASTIC

First published in the UK in 2014 by Scholastic Children's Books
An imprint of Scholastic Ltd
Euston House, 24 Eversholt Street,
London, NW1 1DB, UK
Registered office: Westfield Road, Southam, Warwickshire, CV47 0RA
SCHOLASTIC and associated logos are trademarks and/or registered
trademarks of Scholastic Inc.

Text copyright © Clive Goddard, 2014
The right of Clive Goddard to be identified as the author of this work
has been asserted by him.

ISBN 978 1407 13911 1

A CIP catalogue record for this book is available from the British Library.

Printed and bound by CPI Group (UK) Ltd, Croydon, CR0 4YY
Papers used by Scholastic Children's Books are made from wood grown in
sustainable forests.

1 3 5 7 9 10 8 6 4 2

This is a work of fiction. Names, characters, places, incidents and dialogues are
products of the author's imagination or are used fictitiously. Any resemblance
to actual people, living or dead, events or locales is entirely coincidental.

www.scholastic.co.uk

Thanks to my youngest son Daniel for his ruthless and uncensored opinions while I used his bedtime story to work out the plot. To Amy for her zero tolerance approach to plot holes, and for contributing some of the silly names.

Thanks also to Zöe and Lucy at Scholastic for their ongoing encouragement and editorial sharpness, and to my oldest son Dylan for inventing Fin Tan one day while we were locked out.

PROLOGUE

Fintan Fedora had always wanted to be an explorer. Not just because it rhymed with his name but because the world was full of exciting, weird and exotic places and he wanted to see them all! This wasn't an unusual thing for a fourteen-year-old boy to want but, unlike most fourteen-year-old boys, he actually got to do it.

He was lucky. His family was rich enough to pay for his expeditions and happy enough to let him go on them. He was a pleasant boy, too: friendly, well meaning and generally upbeat about things.

Fintan loved the explorer's life. It was certainly more fun than being stuck at home with his boring family. The Fedora family made cakes, really popular ones like the "Fedora Fancy", which was why they were rich enough to have a large house and a butler. But Fintan didn't really fit in there. His parents thought he was annoying and useless and didn't like him cluttering up the house. Even when he came back from a successful expedition they were only impressed for a short while then couldn't wait for him to go away again. There were also Flavian and Felicity, his rotten older twin brother and sister who made his home life miserable. They teased him, pushed him about and played cruel tricks on him. It was no wonder that Fintan preferred life in the uncharted wilderness to being at home. Sharing a damp tent with a venomous snake was more fun than sharing a house with his venomous brother and sister.

But he had a problem; he was a hopeless, clumsy, accident-prone, chaotic disaster of a human being. Unlike other explorers he couldn't read a map, had no sense of direction, and had an unfortunate habit of breaking everything he touched. He had broken his nose, his arm, his ankle, other people's noses and ankles, and most of the windows in the house. He had fallen into holes, off bridges, and out of hammocks. He frequently lost his way, his passport and his trousers.

Luckily, he had Gribley. Sensible, reliable old Gribley was the Fedora family's butler and always accompanied Fintan on his wild adventures and tried to keep him out of trouble. Together the two of them had crossed stormy oceans, struggled through muddy jungles and paddled down piranha-infested rivers. They had survived unbearable heat, hunger, thirst, and fought off ruthless rivals. Together they had discovered wonderful unseen places and brought back fabulous unknown treasures. The two of them made a great team.

Where would their adventures take them next?

ONE

The plane was descending rapidly through a dense layer of freezing cloud. Fintan pressed his nose against the window and tried to catch a glimpse of the bizarre, rugged landscape below. Iceland looked weird, multicoloured, and wrinkly.

"Look at that!" he said excitedly, grabbing Gribley by his coat sleeve. "It's like some strange alien planet!"

Gribley didn't really want to look. In fact he didn't really want to be there at all.

"No thank you, sir," he said, far more interested in reading his book.

Fintan didn't mind. He knew the expedition was going to be utterly brilliant and he was excited enough for both of them. They were on a quest to discover the mysterious and fabulously rare Icelandic Snowberry. A virtually unknown fruit which, according to *Young Adventurer* magazine, was rumoured only to grow thousands of feet up on the misty slopes of extinct volcanoes. If Fintan was lucky enough to find a living specimen he was going to bring it back to England and make a fortune! He would be known as "Fintan Fedora, the Intrepid Explorer and Discoverer of the Legendary Icelandic Snowberry". It was going to be a difficult and dangerous quest that would take him up mountains and across glaciers, through snow and ice and fire; a journey across strange landscapes of boiling mud and violently hot geysers. He was about as excited as it was possible for a human being to get without actually bursting.

Which explains why he was so disappointed when they got off the plane; the airport souvenir shop was stocked with hundreds of jars of snowberry jam.

TWO

"Morning, loser!" shouted an arrogant voice from the hallway. "Want some toast with snowberry jam for breakfast?"

"*Snow* good talking to him," added another voice, falling apart with mocking laughter. "He's *berry* stupid!"

It was Fintan's horrible older brother and sister, Flavian and Felicity, whose favourite hobby was making fun of him. He had been back home at Fedora Hall for nearly a week now and they were still teasing him about the disastrous Icelandic trip. It looked like it wasn't going to be forgotten in a hurry. The sooner Fintan could get out of the house on another adventure the better.

He did his best to ignore them and made his way

to the kitchen, where Gribley was seated at the table reading a small blue book.

"Morning, Gribs," he said brightly. "Has the postman been yet?"

"He has indeed, sir," announced Gribley, marking his place in the book and getting up from the table.

Fintan rubbed his hands gleefully, knocking over a box of cereal with his elbow. "Brilliant!" he said. "It's *Young Adventurer* magazine day at last!"

Gribley fetched the post and started making the breakfast. He could have let Fintan make his own of course but that often led to one of the boy's little accidents. And it was far too nice a morning to be spoilt by the sound of broken plates and smoke alarms going off. There were still black soot stains under the kitchen cupboards from the time Fintan had set fire to the toaster, and a hole in the worktop where he had melted the kettle.

"Thanks, Gribs," said Fintan as he was presented with a mug of sweet tea and a pile of toast buried in peanut butter.

Things didn't get much better than this. A good breakfast, a sunny day with no school and a whole new magazine to read! All he needed now was for

Flavian and Felicity to be abducted by aliens to make the day perfect. He tore the plastic wrapping from the latest *Young Adventurer* and surveyed the cover. It was an exciting drawing of a fishing boat crew grappling with a giant squid, hacking at its tentacles with axes. Fintan thought it was brilliant!

The rest of the magazine was just as good: an exciting mix of amazing "facts" from around the world and action-packed adventure stories; fabulous stuff about man-eating tigers, mysterious snake-charmers and rumbling volcanoes. There was an excellent article on dog sleds falling into deep crevasses in the Antarctic, and photos of exotic islands where the crabs climbed trees and the local tribes hadn't changed since the Stone Age. There were fantastic colour drawings of extinct giant sloths and armoured pangolins the size of buses. He settled down to read a story about an expedition that headed into the forests of New Guinea and were never seen again. Headhunters were suspected to have eaten them!

"Don't forget to eat your breakfast, sir," reminded Gribley, sitting down again with his little blue book.

"Oh right," said Fintan.

He took a huge mouthful of cold toast. "What's that you're reading, Gribs?"

Gribley was surprised the boy had even noticed he was in the room, let alone that he was holding a book!

"It's a volume of ancient Chinese poetry, sir. *The Song of the Moon Dragon*."

"Oh," said Fintan, immediately losing interest. He didn't like poetry.

"It was written eight hundred years ago by the Great Master of Yin," added Gribley.

Fintan nodded but couldn't think of anything else to say. He knew absolutely nothing about ancient Chinese poetry and was quite happy for it to stay that way. He gulped down some lukewarm tea and returned to a story about two-headed white bats living deep in the caves of Patagonia.

"It is the poet's great unfinished masterpiece, sir," continued Gribley.

"What is?" said Fintan, wondering whether two-headed bats ever bit themselves by mistake.

Gribley sighed. "*The Song of the Moon Dragon*, sir. The book of Chinese poetry which I mentioned a few seconds ago."

"Oh right," said Fintan. "Unfinished. A bit boring then, is it?"

Gribley winced. Sometimes talking to Fintan was like trying to explain ballet dancing to a dog.

"Not at all, sir, it's actually very interesting. The Great Master of Yin was a multi-talented man. As well as being a poet he was also an artist and a sculptor. The great tragedy is that he disappeared before he could finish his finest work. In fact his whole village disappeared. According to legend the village of Yin was a fabulously beautiful place with towering gold pagodas filled with many of the Great Master's treasures. Including the legendary Moon Dragon, itself carved in gold . . . and no one has ever found it."

"Cool," said Fintan, half listening and half looking at a drawing of Bigfoot, who was ten feet tall with shaggy white fur and massive scary teeth.

In the centre pages of the magazine he found an illustrated article about the Great Wall of China.

"Hey, look at this, Gribs," he said. "There's a thing about China in here! Apparently there's a really big old wall there."

Gribley looked up. "Indeed, sir," he said. "The

famous Great Wall of China. I believe it is over six thousand kilometres long."

"Wow," said Fintan, impressed with Gribley's ability to remember astonishing facts. "That must have taken a lot of bricks! Is it anywhere near the place you were talking about?"

Gribley was surprised the boy had even been listening.

"The lost village of Yin, sir?" he said. "I'm afraid Yin has been lost for eight hundred years. No one is even sure where it was to begin with."

"Lost for eight hundred years, eh?" mused Fintan.

Gribley held his breath. There was a look on the boy's face which suggested he was getting one of his dangerous ideas. The sort of idea which usually led to poor old Gribley being dragged away from home on some terrible expedition.

"Well in that case . . ." announced Fintan, closing his magazine, "it's about time someone found it!"

THREE

Less than a week later Fintan was in his room
packing for the great Chinese trek. His parents
had been surprisingly keen on the idea when he
suggested it to them and had happily agreed to pay
for everything. It was almost as if they couldn't wait
to get rid of him! They weren't even put off when
Gribley protested that Yin didn't exist.

Fintan fastened his brand-new explorer's belt
around his jungle shorts and admired himself in the
bedroom mirror. He looked like a proper explorer.
Well, apart from the spotty purple and yellow
socks, anyway.

Gribley had given him a belt with two safety
clips attached. These were meant to keep his
wallet and mobile phone safe. Of course, this

didn't mean they would. Fintan was an expert at losing things.

Mrs Fedora was supervising his packing.

"You'll need plenty of warm vests," she said, selecting a neatly folded pile of them from his wardrobe. "I expect it can get a bit chilly in China, and we don't want you catching a cold, do we?"

"No, Mum," he agreed, while having no intention of taking any vests at all.

Explorers didn't need vests! They didn't need clean clothes every day when they were trudging through the wilderness! And they certainly didn't need smart shirts and ties like the ones his mother had packed in case he went out for a nice meal in the evening.

There was a knock at Fintan's bedroom door and his twin brother and sister sauntered in. Flavian and Felicity strolled over to him smirking as if they were up to something, which they obviously were.

"Hi, Mum," said Felicity brightly. "We thought we'd give little brother a going away present."

"So we got him some nice cakes for the journey," added Flavian, smiling a little too broadly to be taken seriously.

He handed Fintan a box of Fedora Fancies, the bestselling cake assortment made by the family business. Fintan wasn't impressed. There were several hundred boxes of Fedora Fancies in the kitchen cupboard.

"Oh, look!" said his mother. "You like those, don't you? Say thank you to your brother and sister."

"Thank you for the cakes," he mumbled.

Felicity and Flavian stifled a giggle. What their poor little brother didn't know was that they had spent the previous six hours in the shed soaking every single cake in a foul chemical concoction of their own invention. It contained laxatives, mouldy tuna-flavoured cat food, some out-of-date egg mayonnaise, and some unidentified gooey brown stuff they'd scraped out of the bath plughole.

"So you're making poor old Gribley take you to China then, are you?" said Flavian. "Bit selfish, isn't it?"

"Just to find some stupid lost village!" added Felicity, snorting as she spoke. "You couldn't even find a lost sock!"

Fintan frowned. He was fed up with this pair of idiots making fun of him. He'd show them! He'd go and find that lost village of Yin and that statue of the golden Moon Dragon too! What's more he would bring it back and wave it in his stupid siblings' faces. And maybe hit them with it a bit.

"Gribs says he's always wanted to go to China," said Fintan defensively.

"Yeah, but not with you!" laughed Felicity and was joined by her brother in a bout of chortling and high-fiving.

They turned and swaggered out of the room.

"Bye bye, little brother," called Flavian. "Don't forget to bring us back some brilliant presents.

"And enjoy the lovely cakes!" added Felicity through a stream of silly giggles.

"Oh, how nice!" cooed his mother. "Wasn't that nice of them, Fintan?"

Fintan made a reluctant grunting sound. Whatever it was they were doing, he doubted it was nice.

FOUR

The day of the China trek dawned.

"Here we go again, eh, Gribs!" said Fintan as they wandered around the airport. "The great explorers off on another exciting mission!"

"Indeed, sir," muttered Gribley miserably.

They had two hours to spare before their flight so wandered aimlessly around the airport shops looking at fancy luggage and neck pillows. Fintan was asked to leave one of them after knocking over a large display of novelty teddy bears dressed as airline pilots. After this Gribley suggested they should probably give the expensive perfume shop a miss. Fintan was extremely excited so made several trips to the toilet. This also helped to pass quite a lot of time.

Eventually it was time to board. He followed Gribley on to the plane and shuffled down the aisle, hitting several passengers in the face with his backpack.

"You'll need to turn off your phone for the flight, sir," said Gribley. "I believe it interferes with the aeroplane's radar."

"Oh, right," said Fintan, taking his seat and fumbling around for it. It was missing. He reached behind his back and under his bottom in case he was sitting on it. It was still missing.

"Can't find it, Gribs," he said. "That's a mystery!"

"You can't possibly have lost it, sir," said Gribley. "It's clipped to your belt."

"Yeah, but I'm not wearing my belt. I took it off in the—"

Suddenly Fintan remembered where he'd left it. "It's in the toilet!"

A look of despair crept over Gribley's face. They were still in England and the disasters had started already. "What's it doing in there?" he said.

"Well," explained Fintan, "I didn't want my valuable things dangling in the loo, you see, so I took the belt off and hung it on the back of the door. For safekeeping."

Gribley took a deep breath and decided he wasn't going to let it spoil their day. "Not to worry, sir," he said calmly. "I'll ask your father to send over some money, and we can buy a replacement phone. . . Wait, where are you going?"

Fintan was out of his seat and running up the aisle. "Don't worry, Gribs!" he shouted. "I know exactly where it is! Shouldn't take a minute."

"But. . ." began Gribley as he watched Fintan head towards the exit. "There isn't time! The plane is about to take off!"

Fintan wasn't listening. He was too busy apologizing to all the passengers he'd just whacked with his bag again. A flight attendant attempted to persuade Fintan to sit back down but he was out of the door and running down the tunnel before she could stop him.

"I'll be really quick!" he shouted as he disappeared from view.

Gribley sat and waited, anxiously glancing at his watch. A minute passed, then another, followed by five more. There was still no sign of the boy. The cabin crew was given the go-ahead for take-off and began locking the door. Gribley tried to persuade them to wait a little longer but it was too late. The plane began taxiing towards the runway.

Meanwhile in the terminal building Fintan still hadn't found the right toilet. He'd tried three already and none of them had his belt in. One had even been full of girls! An urgent voice kept calling his name over the tannoy system. "Last call for Mr Fedora on the flight to Beijing," it insisted. "Will Mr Fedora please go to the departure gate."

After frantically running the wrong way along a moving walkway he caught sight of the shop with the teddy bears dressed as airline pilots. The toilet was right next to it. He dashed through the door and ran straight into a cleaner, knocking her to the floor.

"Sorry but no one's allowed in here. It's closed," she said, picking herself up.

"But I just need to get my things," said Fintan, breathing hard. "I left them in there."

He pointed to the end cubicle, which now had a yellow and black danger sign placed in front of it.

"Oh no. . . Is someone in there?" he asked.

"It's a suspicious item," explained the cleaner. "So there's a security alert."

"But I just need to get my things!" blurted

Fintan. "I'm in a real hurry! I could miss my fli—"

He was interrupted by the door behind him bursting open and two burly policemen rushing in. They were wearing padded body armour, carrying guns and had matching moustaches.

"Where's the suspect device?" barked one of the men.

"Where's the bomb?" added the other, in case no one knew what a suspect device was.

The cleaner pointed to the locked cubicle. "In that one," she said.

Fintan couldn't believe it. Of all the bad luck in the world his had to be the worst! A bomb? Fancy someone leaving a bomb in the very same toilet cubicle where he'd left his belt!

"Stand aside, please. I'm going to take a look," said the first policeman.

"Stand back," added the second. "I'm going in."

Repeating things in a slightly different way seemed to be his job.

At that exact moment, somewhere out on the runway the plane to China was lifting into the sky with the forlorn face of Gribley pressed against one of the windows.

FIVE

Fintan was sitting alone in the airport terminal feeling sorry for himself. He had his belt back but had just been thoroughly told off by both policemen for wasting their time. They had enough to do without dealing with absent-minded boys causing bomb hoaxes in toilets! Worst of all, the plane had gone without him and there was nothing he could do about it. He switched on his mobile phone to call Gribley and apologize. LOW BATTERY it said then went off again. He'd forgotten to charge it. And anyway, Gribley's phone would be switched off until the plane got to China. This was a problem. For a brief moment Fintan considered calling home to ask his parents what to do, but decided it was a bad idea. They were already convinced he was a hopeless idiot and this would make things even worse. Besides, if his brother and sister knew he'd missed his flight they would never stop teasing him about it. There was nothing else for it; he would have to make his own way to China.

He wandered around the terminal building for a while until he caught sight of a sign saying Help Desk. This was, in more ways than one, a good sign.

"Excuse me," he said to a friendly-looking young woman in a blue uniform. "I'd like to go to China, please."

"Certainly, sir," chirped the woman, who according to her name badge was called Debee. "Would that be Beijing, sir?"

Fintan was pretty sure it would be. He nodded.

"And when would you like to travel?"

"Well, now would be good, please," said Fintan.

"OK, sir, not a problem," trilled Debee and consulted her computer monitor. "I'm afraid you've just missed a flight to Beijing, sir. It departed around ten minutes ago."

"I know!" said Fintan, wondering how Debee knew about this. Had she been watching him?

"There are a few seats available on a flight next Tuesday, sir. Would that be convenient?"

She showed Fintan her computer screen. It was currently a Wednesday, which meant waiting at the airport for nearly a week. That was no good at all.

"Haven't you got anything a bit sooner?" he asked hopefully.

Debee tapped on her keyboard again. "I could get you to Moscow in Russia today, if you like, and you could take a train the rest of the way from there."

This sounded like a much better idea. Fintan liked trains. He liked them a lot more than aeroplanes anyway. He had very fond memories of a childhood train trip to the seaside during which nothing had broken, fallen apart or blown up. It was a wonderful, golden memory.

"Brilliant!" he said. "How much is it? I've got money."

"I'm afraid you can't book it here, sir, but you can probably arrange the Trans-Siberian train journey at that travel agency over there," said Debee, pointing across the terminal with her bright red fingernails. "And of course you'll need to go to that desk over there and arrange yourself a flight to Russia."

Fintan's expression brightened immediately. He wasn't entirely useless after all! He was making alternative travel plans and he was doing it without Gribley's help! He gave Debee a cheery thumbs-up and walked off in the wrong direction.

SIX

As soon as Gribley arrived in China he called Fintan's phone but there was no reply. It was either still lost, had a flat battery or Fintan had dropped it in the toilet again. He checked himself into the hotel and made himself feel at home by remaking the beds properly and correcting the way the curtains hung. Just as he finished polishing the bathroom mirror to his satisfaction, his phone rang. It was an international number which he didn't recognize.

"Hello?" he said.

"Hello!" replied a very distant voice. "Is that you, Gribs?"

Gribley was relieved to hear the familiar voice. "Ah, Master Fintan! How good to hear from you! I trust you are all right, sir?"

"Oh yeah, I'm fine!" said Fintan. "Really sorry about missing the plane and all that. I got a bit lost."

This came as no surprise to Gribley. He'd known the boy to get lost in his own house.

"May I ask where you are calling from?" he said.

"The airport," said Fintan.

Gribley was stunned. "Really, sir?" he said. "You're still at the airport?"

"No, no, not that airport, Gribs! I'm in a different one now."

"I see. In which airport, sir?"

"Er . . . hang on. . ." There was a slight pause as Fintan asked someone to remind him where he was.

"I'm in Ankara."

This, however, was surprising news.

"Ankara?" enquired Gribley. "What are you doing in Ankara?"

"Well, there weren't any more planes to China you see, Gribs, so the woman said I should go to Russia first and then catch a train to China."

Gribley hesitated.

"But Ankara's not in Russia, sir. It's in Turkey."

"Is it?" said Fintan. "Are you sure? They all speak

another language here and I can't read the signs. Hang on. . ."

There was another pause as Fintan spoke to a passer-by.

"Excuse me? Is this Turkey?"

Whoever he had asked must have nodded their head.

"Blimey, Gribs, you know everything!" said Fintan, sounding impressed. "I *am* in Turkey! Never mind, don't you worry about me. I'll get there all right!"

Gribley put his free hand over his eyes. The boy was incredible. He never seemed to run out of ingenious new ways to mess things up.

A beeping noise interrupted the call. He could just about hear Fintan trying to borrow some more Turkish coins when they were abruptly cut off.

SEVEN

Several hours later, after a lot of help from some very kind Turkish people, Fintan finally landed at Moscow airport. He was in Russia at last! Hungry and in desperate need of a comfy bed, he arrived at the immigration desk and held out his passport. A man wearing a very fancy uniform examined his photograph and compared it with the scruffy specimen standing before him. He then flicked through the pages of the passport.

"Where are your proper documents?" he said with a thick Russian accent. "Where is your visa?"

"Pardon?" said Fintan.

"You must have a visa to enter Russia," continued the official.

Fintan was confused. A visor? One of those

peaked cap things you wore to keep the sun out of your eyes? He knew some countries had strange laws but this was just weird! Russia wasn't the sunniest of places, after all.

"Seriously?" he said. "I didn't bring one. I think my mum's got one in the wardrobe at home though. It's a green one for playing tennis."

The immigration officer didn't find this funny. He looked like the sort of person who never found anything funny. He picked up a phone and called for assistance. Two huge men in even fancier uniforms appeared and took it in turns to flick through Fintan's passport. It appeared Russians took the visor thing very seriously.

"I've got sunglasses," said Fintan helpfully. "Is that any good?"

"You come with me, please," said the bigger of the two men and grabbed Fintan by the shoulder.

EIGHT

Meanwhile in China, Gribley was enjoying himself enormously. Beijing was a very old and very cultured city, packed full of centuries of history. He had picked up a free guidebook at the hotel reception and was happily wandering the ancient streets marvelling at the sights. A yellowish haze of cloud and smoke hung over the whole city, making the warm air even more humid and reducing the sun to a vague glow. He took a leisurely stroll through a large, leafy park where middle-aged ladies were dancing and twirling colourful ribbons to loud screechy music. He visited ancient temples and the ruins of the Emperor's richly decorated summer palace. He climbed the worn stone steps to the old drum tower and looked out over the rooftops. It was wonderful. Gribley had read many books about this place but had never imagined he'd actually see it!

He couldn't help feeling a little guilty though. The fact that Fintan wasn't with him had turned out to be something of a blessing. He was in a city he had always wanted to visit; doing all the things he enjoyed doing . . . without having to deal with a single disaster!

NINE

Back in Russia, Fintan had been taken to a small, shabby room with no windows. It was completely empty apart from a grubby table and two plastic chairs. The uniformed man gestured for him to sit, then stood by the door and practised looking mean. Fintan sat. After a minute or two a blonde-haired woman came in and sat opposite Fintan. She was wearing a large furry hat and didn't look very friendly.

"So. . ." she began in an icy cold voice. "You are Mr Fedora, no?"

"No," agreed Fintan, while nodding his head. "I mean yes. I am him. Yes."

She began writing notes on a sheet of paper. "Where did you start your journey?"

"From home," stated Fintan, thinking it was a bit of an obvious question.

The stern-faced woman didn't appear to be amused. "From which country?" she said flatly.

"Oh, I see!" said Fintan. "I started from England."

"And what is the purpose of your visit to Russia?"

"Purpose?" mused Fintan. "Well, because I couldn't get the train from Turkey."

She wrote this down, then looked up with a pained expression on her face. "Turkey? First say you England, now you say Turkey. Which is it?"

"Both," said Fintan, nodding his head. "But I want to go to China."

She sighed and wrote this down, too. "You want to get the train to China, yes?"

"Yes," said Fintan, sounding quite certain. "Well, not really but I have to . . . because I got off the plane."

"Which plane?"

"The one in England."

The woman stopped writing, crumpled up her piece of paper and threw it in the bin.

"Hey, don't worry about it," said Fintan cheerily. "I make mistakes like that all the time! My mum says it's always best to start again with a clean sheet."

Without speaking, the woman got up and left the room looking stunned. Talking to Fintan often had that effect on people.

About an hour later she returned, handed back Fintan's passport and fixed him with a serious gaze. "Now listen carefully," she said. "You are in Russia illegally without a visa so you must be removed. My associate, Sergeant Gogol, will escort you to the train station and make sure that you leave the country at once."

Fintan was relieved to hear this. "Oh good, thanks," he said, smiling broadly. "And if I ever come here again I'll bring loads of visors, honest!"

TEN

Meanwhile, on the other side of the city a different sort of meeting was taking place. Russia's most dangerous one-eyed gangster, Boris "Dead-Eye" Rottervich, had gathered his men together. The four of them were seated around a table in a cold, deserted warehouse, wearing long leather coats and fierce expressions. Above them a single dim light bulb was hanging from the ceiling. And so was an upside-down Chinese man, tied up, blindfolded and dangling by his ankles.

"Tell us what you know!" shouted Dead-Eye Rottervich. "Tell us everything!"

"But I don't know anything, honest!" said the poor dangling man.

"A likely story!" sneered Rottervich. "How did

you know where to find us? Who told you we were here?"

"Your address was written on a piece of paper. I was just following orders!" squealed the man, rotating slowly.

"Whose orders?" barked Rottervich. He really enjoyed interrogating people.

The helpless man whimpered slightly. "My boss's orders. I just do what I'm told!"

"Your boss, eh? Who do you work for?"

"Tasty Wok Restaurant," said the upside-down man. "Quality Chinese Takeaway. Free delivery."

Rottervich went silent for a moment and scowled angrily at his three gang members.

"Which one of you morons ordered a Chinese food delivery to our secret hideout?"

An unshaven man with a flat nose owned up. "Sorry, boss," he said. "That was me. I forgot."

Rottervich whacked him with a piece of rusty pipe.

"Idiot!" he yelled. "How are we supposed to keep this place secret if you're going to give the address to Chinese takeaways? Now get rid of him!"

"Sorry, Mr Rottervich," mumbled the flat-nosed man.

He climbed on to the table and cut the prisoner's ropes, dropping him noisily to the floor.

The gang wasn't supposed to eat Chinese food anyway. Rottervich had banned it since they became involved in a feud with a rival Chinese gang. Known as the 'Knot of Blood' these bitter enemies had been muscling in on their territory and bumping off their men.

"Perhaps now we can get to business?" announced Rottervich as soon as the delivery man had been thrown out of the building.

The rest of the gang rejoined him at the table and handed around the Chinese food. It would be a shame to waste it after all.

"So. . ." continued Rottervich. "Thanks to a prisoner I interrogated earlier. . ."

He paused and glowered at Flat-Nose. "A *proper* prisoner that is . . . not a delivery boy!"

Flat-Nose blushed and stared at his noodles.

"Thanks to my proper prisoner I have learnt some very useful information about our Chinese enemy. For instance, the name of their leader. The boss of the Knot of Blood is a very large, fat man called Fin Tan! We also now know the exact location of his secret hideout!"

"Excellent!" mumbled his men through mouthfuls of chicken chow mien.

Rottervich dumped a metal box on the table. It was full of guns, knives, knuckledusters and fake passports. There was a nasty glint in his one good eye while the fake one was looking sideways at the wall.

"Gentlemen . . ." he announced darkly, "we are going on a little trip to China! That fat swine 'Fin Tan' won't know what hit him!"

The gang looked a bit confused and gaped vaguely at each other.

"Who?" said a really ugly one with a tattooed face.

"Fin Tan!" he barked. "The boss of the Knot of Blood, remember?"

"Oh him," said the men, still chewing their takeaways.

Rottervich despaired. His gang was rubbish.

ELEVEN

Fintan was being driven to the Moscow train station by Sergeant Gogol, who had strict orders to make sure the boy left the country.

"I like your hat," said Fintan, in an attempt to start a conversation. "Nice and furry."

Gogol said nothing and kept his eyes on the road.

"Must be really warm," continued Fintan.

Still nothing. Fintan sat and looked out at the snow-covered city for a while.

"Wish I could have a hat like that," he said. "Seems a shame to come all the way to Russia and not get a nice hat like that."

Just around the corner they passed a bustling open-air market crammed with people.

"Wonder if they sell furry hats there?" mused Fintan as loudly as possible.

Eventually Gogol sighed and stopped the car.

"Five minutes," he said and unlocked Fintan's door.

"Thanks, Mister Goggle," grinned Fintan, stepping out into the crunchy snow.

Gogol led him to a row of stalls selling tourist items. There were plenty of furry hats as well as little snow domes, Russian stars and flags all laid out on a bright red tablecloth. Fintan immediately tried on the biggest, furriest hat there was. It was a bit too big but he loved it anyway.

"Seven hundred rubles," said the woman behind the stall.

"Rubles?" said Fintan. "What are rubles?"

Gogol got out his wallet.

"Russian money," he said in his deep rumbling voice. "It is OK. I will pay for hat."

Seven hundred Rubles wasn't as much as it sounded and he would be able to claim the money back as expenses anyway.

"Really? That's very nice of you, thanks!" grinned Fintan.

As he turned to go back to the car he caught sight of a huge display of brightly painted Russian stacking dolls. The little wooden ones that nest inside each other and get tinier and tinier.

"Oh, look at those things! I bet my mum would love one of those!" he said excitedly.

He selected a big, beautifully painted one with a red headscarf and rosy-cheeked face.

"Yes, very good for mother!" agreed the woman behind the stall. "Do you have sister? Also very good for sister," she added, hoping to sell him two of them.

Fintan looked horrified at the thought. Why on earth would he want to buy a present for Felicity?

"Can I get one of these too, please, Mr Goggle?" he asked, smiling what he hoped was a nice smile. "I'll pay you back, honest!"

Gogol frowned but paid for the doll anyway, making sure he got a receipt for it.

"Brilliant! Thanks, Mr Goggle!" said Fintan gratefully.

These Russian police people were really nice! He crammed the big furry hat on his head and securely stuffed the doll into his backpack. Unfortunately, he also securely stuffed the corner of the stall's tablecloth into his backpack. As he walked away, the tablecloth came with him followed by everything on it. The stall's entire stock crashed noisily to the ground. Hundreds of wooden dolls and glass snow domes hit the concrete, burst open and flew apart. The stall owner screamed in horror. Fintan apologized repeatedly while poor Sergeant Gogol sighed and got out his wallet again.

An hour later they arrived at the railway station. Gogol looked pale and exhausted and his overcoat pockets were full of crumpled receipts. He still couldn't believe he had spent thirty-eight thousand rubles in one afternoon while taking a boy to the station!

As they arrived at the platform Fintan could barely hide his excitement. Waiting for him there was the enormous, silver Trans-Siberian Express: the train which would take him all the way to China!

"Wow! Is this my train?" he asked, peering along it and counting the carriages.

Gogol nodded weakly.

"This is going to be great!" added Fintan. "Thank you for looking after me, Mr Goggle."

He shook the man's limp hand and climbed happily aboard.

All along the platform dozens of other travellers were also boarding the train. Among them were four nasty-looking men in long leather coats. They had guns in their pockets, knives in their boots and murder on their minds. It appeared Fintan was sharing his great Trans-Siberian trek with the dreaded "Dead-Eye" Rottervich.

TWELVE

"It takes *how long* to get to China?" gasped Fintan in shocked disbelief.

"Seven days," repeated the train guard.

Fintan couldn't believe it.

"Seven days?" he said. "But that's nearly a week!"

If he was going to be stuck there for a week he should probably make himself at home. His compartment was surprisingly spacious and quite comfy, too. After a short struggle he worked out how to fold his seat into a bed, then found the reading light and put his feet up. He had brought the latest copy of *Young Adventurer* magazine with him as well as plenty of peanut butter sandwiches, so he wouldn't be bored. The week was probably going to fly by!

The train sped on through open countryside dotted with distant gold-domed buildings.

Things were actually turning out pretty well. Being on a train was much better than being on a boring old aeroplane! Imagine having to go all the way to China crammed into an uncomfortable little seat next to a tiny window with a rubbish view. All those hours of not being able to stand up and stretch your legs and having to eat your dinner off a plastic tray. He had this brilliant compartment all to himself.

Before he knew it the sun had gone down over the snow-capped Russian hills and he was ready for a good night's sleep. He climbed under a grey woolly blanket and switched out the light. Train travel was great!

In the middle of the night Fintan was awoken by a dim light shining in through his window blind. The train had come to a halt at one of the many stations on its route. There was a hushed fumbling noise in the corridor as new passengers came quietly aboard. It all felt strangely exciting. It was a slow but wonderfully relaxing way to travel.

Then his compartment door slid open. A huge Chinese man squeezed in and dumped his suitcase on the opposite seat. He must have been nearly seven feet tall and was built like a wrestler.

"Excuse me," said Fintan, sitting up in his bed. "I think you've made a mistake. This is compartment number five. This is my room."

The man didn't seem to speak any English.

"*Wrong room*," continued Fintan, pronouncing the words as clearly as he could.

"*Wu*," said the man and held up five fingers in translation.

"Woo?" said Fintan, wondering why the man was making ghost noises. "No! This is number five! See, it's written on the door there. Whereas your ticket . . ." he took the man's ticket from his hand and read it, ". . . is for room number . . . five."

"*Wu*," repeated the enormous man, sitting down heavily on his bunk and smiling broadly.

"Oh, right," conceded Fintan. It looked like he was sharing the room after all. Maybe that was why there were two bunks.

"I'm Fintan. What's your name?" he said, shaking the man's big slab of a hand.

"Dong," said the enormous man.

"Dong?" said Fintan, fighting the urge to giggle. It was the silliest name he'd ever heard.

"I'm Fintan," he replied, biting his lip and trying to keep a straight face.

The man stared at him and laughed a very loud and unashamed laugh. "Fin Tan?" he repeated. "You Fin Tan? He ha haaa!"

Fintan couldn't understand what was so funny. There was nothing wrong with his name. It was nowhere near as silly as Dong, anyway!

The uproarious laughter was interrupted by the door sliding open again.

Two more Chinese men bundled in clutching grubby suitcases. Things were getting even sillier.

"Sorry, we're full up in here!" announced Fintan, getting up and waving his arms about.

The men looked confused and double-checked their tickets. They were also booked into compartment number five.

"Wu," they both insisted.

The two new men folded down upper bunks which Fintan hadn't even realized were there and began finding places to store their belongings. For a few chaotic minutes there were elbows and knees and suitcases everywhere and the compartment filled with the smell of sweaty shoes being taken off. Once settled, the three Chinese men introduced themselves to each other. Then Dong pointed at Fintan. "Fin Tan," he said with barely controlled mirth. For some reason the others found this equally hilarious.

The laughter continued for at least half an hour. Occasionally they pretended to be afraid of him and cowered behind each other.

Fintan sat back on his bunk. Oh well, he thought, trying to look on the bright side, perhaps it would be nice to have some company on the long journey. He crawled under his blanket and tried to go back to sleep.

THIRTEEN

The following morning "Dead-Eye" Rottervich and his gang were gathered in the train's dining car drinking coffee and eating pancakes. They had the whole place to themselves.

"Someone clear away all that rubbish," ordered Rottervich, pointing to the mess of dirty cups and plates on the table. "I want to show you something."

Very carefully he placed his briefcase on the table and opened it as gently as possible. His gang all peered inside. The case contained nothing but a brightly painted Russian stacking doll.

They looked puzzled.

"Why did you bring a doll, boss?" asked a man with a neck as thick as a bull's.

A nasty smile spread across Rottervich's face, and his fake eye shone in the morning light.

"Ah!" he said. "This is a present for Mr Fin Tan and the Knot of Blood."

The gang didn't understand. A present for the Knot of Blood? But they're the enemy! What was the boss thinking?

"This is no ordinary doll," continued Rottervich, wagging a finger. "This is a very special doll. With a big surprise inside!"

His men still looked blank so he thought he'd better spell it out.

"When you take it apart . . . doll by doll . . . and you reach smallest doll . . . big surprise!"

He grinned, splayed out his fingers and made a quiet "kaboom" noise. Still no reaction. The gang just stared blankly at him.

"There is bomb in middle!" sighed Rottervich, wishing he had recruited slightly less stupid henchmen.

Finally the gang understood and laughed darkly.

"Ah! Good plan, boss," said the bull-necked man. "But how are we going to give it to them? The Knot of Blood won't trust a present from us!"

"We find someone else to deliver it, of course," continued Rottervich. "Someone who looks innocent and trustworthy. A gullible idiot."

Just at that moment Fintan walked into the dining car and tripped over his shoelace.

"Very good plan, boss," repeated Bull-Neck.

FOURTEEN

Fintan seated himself in a comfortable red leather chair and gazed at his impressive surroundings. The dining car was really posh. It had white linen tablecloths with vases of flowers and the windows had fancy curtains. A smiling, smartly dressed waiter appeared and handed him a menu.

"Thank you," said Fintan happily.

Things were looking up again. The menu looked great but the prices were all in Russian rubles which he didn't understand. He took out one of the Chinese banknotes which Gribley had given him.

"Excuse me," he said, waving it at the waiter. "What can I get for this?"

The waiter immediately stopped smiling.

"Nothing," he said curtly. "Chinese money no good. Only Russian rubles."

"Oh," said Fintan, feeling very disappointed. He emptied the contents of his pockets on to the table. He had about three pounds fifty in loose change, a few Brazilian and Icelandic coins, an expired library card, a matchbox with a dead moth in it and a crumpled bus ticket. He looked up at the waiter hopefully but the man shook his head.

"Can I just have a glass of water then, please?" said Fintan.

For a while he sat and stared sadly out of the window. Then he noticed the scary-looking group of men at the other end of the carriage. For some reason they were all staring at him as if they had just thought of a brilliant idea. One of them appeared to be beckoning him over.

"You . . . boy," called the man in a rough Russian accent.

Fintan looked around. There was no one else there.

"Who, me?" he said.

The man nodded and forced a big smile with his crooked gold teeth. Fintan walked slowly to their table, feeling a bit nervous.

"Sit, please," said the scary Russian man.

Fintan sat. He couldn't help noticing the man had a very unrealistic glass eye which was looking in the wrong direction. He tried not to stare at it.

"I am Mr Rottervich," announced his host, patting himself on his leather-coated chest. "I am, er . . . businessman. These gentlemen are my business associates."

The other three men nodded in agreement. They were all wearing long leather coats and had chunky gold chains around their necks. Fintan thought they must be rock stars or rappers or something.

"Pleased to meet you," said Fintan a little nervously.

"So. . ." continued Mr Rottervich. "You are going to China, yes?"

Fintan nodded, a little distracted by the delicious smell of food coming from the Russians' leftovers.

"We are also going there to visit . . . er, friends."

A loud gurgling sound came from Fintan's stomach.

"You hungry, yes?" asked Rottervich in a deep, rumbling voice.

"Starving," admitted Fintan. "I've only got Chinese money so they won't let me buy anything."

The one-eyed gangster smiled a strange oily smile.

"Ah, this is not a problem," he announced. "We will buy you some good Russian food. Anything you like!"

Fintan felt a surge of happiness. This was so great! Complete strangers being nice to him for no obvious reason.

"Really?" he said. "Thanks ever so much! That's so kind!"

Rottervich waved his hand modestly. "It is nothing! Small favour for our new friend."

He clicked his fingers and barked something to the waiter. An hour later the gangster was beginning to regret his generosity. Fintan had eaten everything on the menu and was working his way through his second dessert.

"You are full now, yes?" enquired Rottervich hopefully.

Fintan patted his belly. "Pretty well stuffed actually, thanks!" he said.

This was fairly obvious. It looked like he'd swallowed a beach ball.

"So. . ." continued the gangster, relieved the

eating was finally over. "We have done you a favour. Now you do us a favour, OK?"

A little later Fintan was back in his compartment digging through his rucksack for the painted Russian doll he had got for his mum. It was a strange coincidence but the nice Russian men had just given him one which was almost identical! They had asked him to deliver it to a business associate of theirs in China. Mr Rottervich had said he was too shy to deliver the present himself and had written the name and address down for him. Who would have thought such a scary-looking man as Rottervich could be so sensitive and caring?

Bizarrely, the Chinese man's name was Fin Tan! It was so similar to his own name that it had caused all the Russians much hilarity. They had fallen around laughing and slapped the table for several minutes.

After a lot of rummaging Fintan located his mum's doll at the bottom of his bag and pulled it out. The Russians had made him promise not to open Fin Tan's present so he just compared the outsides. It was remarkable. They both had the same glossily painted red headscarf, the same yellow shawl with pink flowers and the same rosy-cheeked face.

"Fancy that!" he muttered to himself. "Almost identical!"

In fact the only real difference between them was that one had five little dolls inside it while the other had four dolls and a deadly bomb. Fintan didn't know this, of course, so he happily stuffed them both into his bag.

FIFTEEN

For the next three days very little happened. Fintan spent his days gazing out of the window as the train weaved its way across eastern Russia and through the snowy wastes of Siberia. Eventually they crossed the border into China. Fintan woke early and returned to the window hoping to see some wild pandas galloping about. There weren't any around yet but the scenery was certainly different. There were pagoda-shaped buildings, strange unreadable signs and hundreds and hundreds of Chinese people! It was all very exciting. And being in China meant that Fintan could finally spend his Chinese money in the dining car!

He made his way along the train and eagerly took a seat. The menu had changed too which was great because he liked Chinese food even more than he liked Russian food and almost as much as he liked peanut butter sandwiches. Sitting at the next table were three Chinese people dressed all in black whom he hadn't seen before. Two were thuggish-looking men with shaven heads and masses of tattoos covering their arms. One of the men even seemed to have had his teeth sharpened to little points. He looked like a shark! The third person was probably a woman but it was difficult to tell. There was something about her that turned Fintan's blood cold. Her face was craggy and lumpy and she had teeth like broken piano keys. He'd seen prettier warthogs.

Suddenly the terrifying woman noticed him staring.

"You!" she snapped, pointing a bony finger at him. "Why do you look at me, boy?"

"Sorry," mumbled Fintan, feeling a bit embarrassed.

He gestured towards a squiggly Chinese character inked on to her forearm and pretended to be interested in it.

"I like your tattoos," he said, even though he didn't. "What does that one say?"

"That is my name," announced the warthog-faced woman. "Fang. It means beautiful."

"Does it?" said Fintan, raising his eyebrows and trying not to snigger.

She jabbed a dangerously sharp fingernail at him again. "What is your name, boy?"

"Me? My name's Fintan."

There was a brief stunned silence. Like the Russian men, they found it ridiculously amusing.

"Fin Tan?" squealed Fang in a high-pitched voice.

The other two fell about in hysterics, too, and thumped their fists on the table as tears streamed from their eyes.

"Fin Tan!" yelled Sharky, as if it was the funniest thing he'd ever heard.

"Have you heard of him then?" asked Fintan.

This question caused even more hilarity. The three of them roared and doubled up with laughter.

"Heard of him?" screeched Fang, wiping tears from her eyes. "He's our boss!"

Fintan couldn't believe his luck. Of all the millions of people who lived in China he had just met three who knew Fin Tan! Better still, they actually worked for him!

"No way!" he said excitedly. "I've got a present for him. Hang on, I'll go and get it."

A couple of minutes later he returned with the stacking doll and proudly handed it over.

"Could you give him this, please?"

Fang turned it around admiringly in her hands. "Ah, Russian doll," she said. "Very kind gift!"

"It's from Russia," explained Fintan helpfully.

Fang nodded, but was confused. "Why do you have gift for Fin Tan?"

Fintan felt a bit uncomfortable. It didn't seem right to be taking the credit for someone else's kindness.

"I shouldn't really tell you this ..." he said, leaning in confidentially, "but it's not actually from me at all. It's from his friend, Mr Rottervich."

Fang stopped smiling.

"I met him on the train, you see, and he said he was too shy to take it himself. Don't tell him I said so, will you?" said Fintan with a friendly wink.

"Rottervich?" growled the woman, growing very serious.

"Yeah," said Fintan. "What a nice chap, eh?"

Suddenly Fang shrieked something Fintan didn't understand and handed the stacking doll to the shark-toothed man. The whole Chinese gang leapt up in a state of panic, knocking their cups and plates to the floor. Sharky held the doll at arm's length while the other man wrenched open the window. After a lot of pointing and shouting the doll was hurled furiously outside.

Fintan was stunned. "Didn't you like it?" he said.

That evening Fintan bumped into Fang again walking along the train corridor. It seemed she had been looking for him.

"Boy," she hissed, opening a black leather case. "You must take this, please."

Fintan found himself holding a very fancy bottle of Chinese rice wine with elaborate writing on it.

"This is a gift for Mr Rottervich," whispered Fang. "Very special and valuable Chinese delicacy. I am also shy so please do not say it is from me. Tell him it is from you."

"Wow. That's really sweet!" smiled Fintan and tapped the side of his nose in a confidential manner. "Don't worry. I won't tell."

He was finding all this anonymous gift-giving very touching. Despite their shark-teeth, broken noses and tattoos these people were genuinely nice! It just went to show how you shouldn't judge someone by their appearance!

SIXTEEN

The next morning Fintan woke up in a great mood. It was the seventh and final day of his Trans-Siberian journey and in a few hours he would be reunited with good old Gribley. He arrived at the dining car extra early and extra hungry for breakfast. Rottervich and his gang were already there drinking steaming cups of coffee.

"Morning," chirped Fintan as he walked by, then suddenly remembered the gift he was supposed to deliver. This might be his last chance.

"Oh, I've got something for you!" he announced, turning to go and fetch it. "Don't go away!"

He popped back to compartment number five, happy to be running the errand. In fact it was little things like this that had made the long journey bearable. Without his lovely new Russian and Chinese friends it would have been unbelievably boring.

Unfortunately compartment number five was an absolute mess and he had no idea where he'd put the fancy bottle of wine. Dong and the other two were still sprawled on their bunks, snoring and farting contentedly. A whole week's worth of dirty socks, underpants and sweaty vests were strewn over every surface, as well as crumpled newspapers and empty noodle pots. It smelt revolting, too.

The bottle must have rolled under something, thought Fintan, peering beneath his bunk, but it wasn't there. He searched the other bunks, the floor and everywhere else he could think of but there was no sign of it.

After about half an hour of scrabbling through the mess he gave up. This was weird. It had completely disappeared! He would just have to give Mr Rottervich something else instead. But what? He opened his backpack and tipped everything out. There was a stacking doll but that was for his mum. There was a damp towel, a pair of pyjamas, a pair of grubby boots, and many other things that would make a terrible present. Finally he found a very bent box of Fedora Fancies; the cakes his horrible brother and sister had given him.

"Oh well," he said to himself while trying to unbend the box. "These'll have to do."

He ran back to the dining car. Luckily the Russians were still there.

"Here, I got you these," wheezed a slightly out-of-breath Fintan and handed them the box of Fedora Fancies. "It's nothing special. Just some English cakes . . . from England. It's my family's recipe."

Unfortunately, it was a bit more than the normal family recipe. These were the cakes that Flavian and Felicity had soaked in an assortment of revolting things. The Russians passed them around, nodded their appreciation and happily tucked into them.

"Very good," said Rottervich, spraying crumbs and bits of pink icing as he spoke.

"Oh, by the way," added Fintan brightly. "You'll never guess who I saw on the train yesterday!"

Rottervich shrugged, busily chewing his third Fedora Fancy.

"A Chinese lady called Fang. She works for your friend, Mr Fin Tan!"

All four Russian men suddenly looked very tense.

"Fang is on the train?" blurted Rottervich, spitting out a large mouthful of cake.

It seemed they were already familiar with her.

"I know! Pretty amazing coincidence, eh?" continued Fintan cheerily. "Anyway, it means I won't have to deliver the present now, because I gave it to her instead!"

Rottervich almost choked. "What?" he rasped, sounding horrified.

Fintan stopped himself. If they knew she'd thrown it out of the window, they might get a bit upset. So he decided to improvise.

"She loved it!" he announced. "She said Fin Tan will be very pleased!"

The glass-eyed man looked dubious.

"I watched her open it up and everything!" continued Fintan, making it up as he went along. "She took all the dolls out and put them in a little row."

There was an awkward silence as the Russians exchanged dark glances. It looked as if they didn't believe him. Rottervich stared right into Fintan's face. Well, one of his eyes did anyway. The other one was looking out of the window. "You are lying, boy!" he said in a deep, scary voice.

Fintan was taken aback. How on earth could they know?

"I'm not lying!" he lied.

Rottervich's expression suggested he still didn't believe him. It also suggested he didn't feel very well. His mouth had suddenly gone from a snarl to a grimace and he was drooling like a dog. He clutched his stomach, which had started making peculiar noises as if something were alive in there. Then his face turned a sickly shade of grey. Fintan glanced around the table and noticed that the entire gang was groaning and rubbing their swollen bellies. The bull-necked man had bent over double and was emitting some abnormally loud gurgles. It was the worst outbreak of indigestion Fintan had ever seen! But it couldn't have come at a better time; it meant nobody was talking about the stacking doll any more!

All four men stood up clutching their churning stomachs and lurched away towards the nearest toilet. An ugly fight broke out to see who could get there first. Bull-Neck wrenched the door open but was knocked down and trampled underfoot. Rottervich thumped Flat-Nose in the face then tripped over the fourth who was writhing around on the floor. It wasn't a pretty sight. Eventually Rottervich got to the toilet first and hurriedly locked himself in. A terrifyingly loud squirty noise shuddered through the carriage and rattled all the glass in the windows.

At that precise moment the train began pulling into a station. For the other three men it was perfect timing. Before the train had even come to a halt they opened the door and leapt out. Fintan watched them through the window as they frenziedly dropped their trousers, shuffled across the platform and disappeared into the bushes.

Well that was weird! he thought to himself. *It must have been something they ate.*

A few minutes passed and the men didn't reappear. Even when the whistle blew and the train began to leave without them they remained squatting in the bushes. *Well that was weird . . .* thought Fintan

The train's next stop was the city of Beijing. The capital of China and the end of the line. Fintan crammed all his possessions back into his rucksack and folded up his bunk. On the floor beneath it he found three odd socks, a crumpled copy of *Young Adventurer* magazine and the lost bottle of Chinese wine.

He picked it up and wondered what to do with it. It was too late to give it to Mr Rottervich now. He was still in the toilet shouting at anyone who dared knock on the door and the other three men had been left behind.

Oh well, he thought to himself while stuffing it in a carrier bag with the dirty socks. *It'll make a nice present for Gribley!*

SEVENTEEN

As soon as Fang arrived home she switched on her TV to catch the news headlines. And it was excellent news! Three Russian men had been arrested at a train station for using the bushes as a public toilet. One of them, a massive, tattooed bully of a man with a bite taken out of one ear, was called Veronica Twiddle from Basingstoke. At least, that's what his passport said. Unsurprisingly, this had made the police a bit suspicious so they had taken the men in for questioning. It turned out that they were all travelling with stolen documents and were extremely dangerous, wanted criminals! There was also a news report from Beijing station about another man who had refused to come out of the toilet when his train reached the end of the line.

Railway staff had been forced to take the door off its hinges and pull the man out.

A huge smile erupted across Fang's horrible face. The poisoned wine must have worked! Her enemies had been defeated and the Knot of Blood had won! She immediately picked up the phone and rang her boss.

When the call came through Fin Tan was lounging in his armchair with two cigarettes stuffed into his fat mouth. He shouted for one of his servants to bring the gold-plated telephone over so he wouldn't have to get up. He was a vast, lumbering ox of a man: massively overweight and completely bald apart from a few strands of hair stuck down with sweat.

"What?" he wheezed rudely into the phone.

"Mr Fin Tan, sir, I have good news!" said Fang.

She suggested her boss turn on his TV and see for himself. Fin Tan tuned in just in time to see a very ill-looking Boris Rottervich being dragged away by police, shouting and screaming and draped in toilet paper.

"We are victorious at last!" announced Fang, then went on to explain how it had all had happened. Fin

Tan was delighted, especially when he learned that the Russian gang had been defeated by a young boy who shared his own name. This seemed like a very good omen so he lit himself another two cigarettes to celebrate.

"Excellent work, Madam Fang!" he coughed into the phone. "We must reward this boy for his bravery. See that he is made an honorary member of the Knot of Blood!"

EIGHTEEN

"Master Fintan, sir!" said Gribley as he spotted the scruffy-looking boy waiting on the platform. "A pleasure to see you again."

Fintan was overjoyed. "Hey, great to see you too, Gribs!" he announced and flung out his arms in greeting.

Gribley shook the boy's hand to avoid an embarrassing man-hug. It may have been an emotional reunion but there was no need to let proper standards slip.

"I trust you had an enjoyable journey?" he asked.

"Yeah, great," said Fintan, hoisting his bag on to his back. "Bit boring though."

They walked off together through the chaotic crowd. Thousands of people with thousands of bags flooded around them like a storm tide, shoving and barging each other.

"The city traffic can be rather difficult, sir," said Gribley as they emerged into the station car park, "so I have rented an appropriate vehicle."

Fintan stopped by a large red limousine. "Is this it?" he asked.

Gribley, looking a little awkward, handed him a crash helmet and gestured towards the small moped next to it.

"Wow! Brilliant!" said Fintan.

This was better than a boring old limo any day! They clambered aboard and wobbled unsteadily out into the surging traffic. Fintan had never been on the back of a moped before, nor had he seen anything like the chaotic Beijing traffic. He hung on tightly and gaped at the bizarre assortment of cars, trucks and bikes; all overloaded, honking their horns and spewing out choking fumes. It felt like being thrown into the middle of a stampeding herd of cattle. The city was a jumbled mixture of crumbling old temples and modern concrete tower blocks with neon signs written in Chinese symbols. It was all very bewildering!

"That was seriously cool!" said an obviously excited Fintan as they arrived at their hotel. "So, how are you, Gribs? What've you been up to?"

Gribley felt slightly embarrassed to admit it but he'd been having a fabulous time! He coughed awkwardly into his hand.

"Well . . ." he muttered, "I've mostly been enjoying the delights of the ancient city, sir. I've done some sightseeing and have been learning the language. It really is a most interesting place. The culture, the history, the architecture, the opera. . ."

Fintan nodded and smiled politely but it didn't sound like his sort of thing at all. They checked into the hotel and took the lift upstairs with Gribley continuing to describe some of the marvellous things he had seen and experienced.

"And have you found out where Yin is yet?" asked Fintan hopefully as they reached their room.

"I'm afraid not, sir," said Gribley. "Yin is a lost village. It could be absolutely anywhere."

Fintan wasn't going to be put off by a little problem like that. It had taken him a week to get there and he was itching to get out and start exploring!

"Oh go on, Gribs!" he pleaded, smiling one of his

more convincing smiles. "It'll be a real adventure! Me and you on the motorbike zooming through China looking at the mountains and pandas and stuff!"

Gribley still wasn't convinced. "But we have no idea where to look, sir! And China is an extraordinarily large country."

He gestured towards a stack of brochures he had laid out on Fintan's bedside table.

"Perhaps we could just enjoy some of its popular attractions instead, sir? The Great Wall, for example? Or the Ming Tombs or the famous Terracotta Warriors?"

Fintan wrinkled up his nose at this suggestion. The very idea! He was an explorer not a tourist!

NINETEEN

Meanwhile Boris "Dead-Eye" Rottervich was having a terrible time. He was sitting in a grubby toilet at the police station and feeling really sorry for himself. He wasn't used to this sort of misery and discomfort. He was used to causing misery and discomfort to other people! How had everything gone so horribly wrong? How had Russia's most terrible and feared gangster been reduced to this shameful situation? He didn't even have a gang any more!

It was a mystery. How could they all have fallen ill at exactly the same time? What had they all eaten? A nasty squiggling noise shuddered through his aching stomach and his mouth suddenly tasted like a rancid Fedora Fancy. His eyes widened with a terrible realization. It was the cakes! That annoying little English kid had poisoned them. He must have been working for the Knot of Blood all the time! Which explained why he had lied about giving the stacking doll to Fang!

A wave of fury flooded through him, closely followed by a wave of nausea. That horrible, scruffy-haired little English boy had tricked him. Rottervich gritted his teeth and vowed that he would hunt the boy down and get his revenge! Unfortunately that might have to wait a while. At least until he managed to escape from police custody and was able to stay out of the toilet for more than five minutes.

TWENTY

After a good night's sleep Fintan was up early and eager to begin exploring. They were way behind schedule already! He was lying on the floor staring at a map of China and doodling little pandas around the edges.

"So where d'you think we should start looking, Gribs?" he asked. "Any ideas?"

Gribley sighed and turned the map the right way up.

"As I believe I mentioned several times before departure, sir, no one knows. Unless of course—"

He stopped himself, feeling a little reluctant to continue. It was just a silly myth after all and he didn't want Fintan getting excited for nothing.

"Unless what?" asked Fintan.

"Well . . . unless the rumour is true of course, sir. There are some people who believe there is a clue to the village's location hidden in the poetry."

Fintan liked the sound of this enormously. "A hidden clue? Really? That's brilliant! Can I see your book then?"

"It's not actually printed in the book, Master Fintan," explained Gribley. "It's supposed to be hidden somewhere in the original manuscript, which I believe is kept at the old library in Len Ding."

He pointed to a remote dot on the map surrounded by mountains and mile upon mile of thick forest.

"Many scholars and historians have studied it over the centuries but found nothing."

"Oh, right," said Fintan casually. "Well, I could pop in and have a quick look, if you like."

Gribley was taken aback.

"I don't mean to be rude, sir," he said, "but . . . some of the greatest minds in history have tried to solve the riddle of Yin. And they have all failed. What makes you think you might succeed by 'popping in to have a quick look'?"

Fintan shrugged but still managed to look ridiculously optimistic.

"Dunno," he said. "They could've missed something, couldn't they?"

Gribley raised a surprised eyebrow.

"You do realize they are written in Chinese, don't you, sir?"

"Oh yeah," said Fintan, not even slightly discouraged. "In that case I'd better take my phrase book then."

He tipped the contents of his rucksack out on to his bed and noticed a yellow plastic bag. It contained some dirty socks, and Fang's fancy bottle of rice wine.

"Hey, Gribs," he announced, having quickly thrown out the dirty socks, "I got you a little present!"

But before he could hand it over, the phone rang and Gribley answered it.

"Master Fintan's room," he said.

A surprised look appeared on his face. He hung up and turned to Fintan.

"That was the hotel reception, sir," he said. "Apparently there is a gentleman downstairs who wishes to take you to lunch."

"Really?" said Fintan. "Who on earth can that be?"

Together they took the lift to the ground floor to find out. Standing by the reception desk was a shaven-headed Chinese man with shark-like pointed teeth.

"Oh, hello," said Fintan. "Fancy seeing you here!"

Sharky looked completely out of place in the hotel's refined surroundings. Gribley looked absolutely horrified.

"Do you know this . . . person, sir?" he hissed into Fintan's ear.

"Yeah, don't worry, Gribs," said Fintan happily. "I met him on the train."

The gangster gestured towards the street where a large car stood with its engine running.

"Please," he said. "Madam Fang is waiting in the restaurant for you."

Gribley gripped Fintan's arm. "Are you quite sure this is a good idea, sir?" he whispered.

"Don't see why not, Gribs!" said Fintan casually. "We both like Chinese food, don't we!"

Before Gribley knew what was happening, they

were both being ushered into a shiny, chauffeur-driven car and driven away.

The restaurant was a very expensive-looking place draped with sumptuous purple and gold fabrics and lit by elaborate paper lanterns. Fang was seated at a large table surrounded by about a dozen terrifying-looking men, all wearing Knot of Blood tassels. They were the only customers there, as everyone else had presumably run away. The waiters looked as if they wanted to as well. Fintan was escorted to the table and the gang got respectfully to their feet, bowing slightly. They offered him a seat right at the head of the table.

"Master Fintan, sir," said Fang. "We wish to thank you for your kind services."

"What services?" said Fintan, happily taking his seat.

Fang assumed he was just being modest.

"You gave Mr Rottervich our special gift, of course," she said. "We are all most grateful."

"Oh right!" said Fintan, tucking a napkin into his collar and preparing to eat.

Then it dawned on him. He hadn't given Mr

Rottervich the bottle of wine at all. Worse still, he had brought it with him! The yellow plastic bag was still in his hand. Hurriedly he shoved it under the table, hoping no one would notice.

"Oh, and this is my friend, Gribley," he said, quickly changing the subject.

The gang bowed again and ordered the waiter to fetch another chair. Gribley was squeezed in next to Fintan with a very uneasy expression on his face. He didn't like the look of these shaven-headed, tattooed people at all.

"Master Fintan, sir," he whispered, leaning in closely, "I think these people may be gangsters."

"Really?" said a surprised Fintan.

His idea of a gangster wore a big hat, smoked a cigar and looked like Al Capone.

Fang ordered course after course of strange exotic dishes. Fintan had no idea what most of them were but was happy to try the lot. There were huge bowls of lumpy brown things, strange little transparent parcels and bizarre rubbery sea creatures glistening with ruby red sauce. Unfortunately there were no knives or forks. Fintan had never eaten with chopsticks before so he held one in each hand and attempted to stab the food with the pointy ends.

To avoid embarrassment Gribley showed him the correct way to do it, one-handed. This, however, turned out to be even worse. Frowning with concentration, Fintan gripped his chopsticks really tightly and edged them towards the bowl. There was a loud clicking noise as they twisted out of his grip and flew forcefully in different directions. One pierced a paper lantern and broke the bulb while the other flew across the table and wedged itself up a Chinese man's nostril.

Everyone laughed. Well, everyone except Gribley and the poor man with a chopstick up his nose. Fang shouted for the waiter to bring a spoon. It would take the poor boy days to eat his dinner with chopsticks, and there was a possibility that someone might lose an eye.

More and more food was brought to the table. The gang ate noisily and messily and talked with their mouths full which made Gribley even more uncomfortable.

After an hour of non-stop face-stuffing Fang got to her feet and gestured for Fintan to stand up, too. She made a short speech in Chinese then raised her glass and proposed a toast. Gribley got out his phrase book and tried to work out what was being said. It was something about a heroic boy and deadly poison! He decided it was probably time for them to leave.

"To Fintan," chorused the gang, then drained their glasses.

Gribley stood up to lead the boy away but Fang hadn't finished yet. She produced an intricately braided red silk tassel which she hung around Fintan's neck. It was apparently a great honour. Only trusted gang members were allowed to wear the "Knot of Blood". Fintan thought it was something that you dangled from curtains, but he liked it anyway.

"Cor, cheers!" he said. "That's really nice."

The waiters immediately refilled everyone's glass and another toast followed.

"Fintan!" they all said again.

"We really must be going, sir," hissed Gribley, grabbing the boy's sleeve and heading hurriedly towards the door.

"Oh, OK," said Fintan reluctantly. "Bye, everybody. Thanks for the nice dinner."

As soon as they got outside a very relieved Gribley began looking for a taxi while Fintan began looking for his yellow carrier bag. He'd left it under his chair. If Fang found Rottervich's gift she would know he'd not actually delivered it and she might be a bit upset. And he might have to give the red knotty thing back!

"Just a sec, Gribs," he said. "I forgot something."

He dashed back inside but it was too late. One of the waiters had already found the fancy bottle and was pouring some into everyone's glass. For a moment it looked like he was in big trouble but luckily Fang hadn't noticed.

"Young Fin Tan!" she said happily, holding up her glass.

"Young Fin Tan!" agreed the gang and merrily gulped down their wine.

Suddenly Fang crumpled back on to her chair as if she'd been shot with a tranquillizer dart. She stared around with a weird look on her face, then tipped her head back and went very quiet. The rest of the gang looked a bit odd, too. Some of them made grunting noises, went grey and fell face first into their empty dishes. No one moved. Apart from a craggy-faced old man who slid off his chair and thumped on to the floor. Fintan smothered a laugh. He'd never seen people get so drunk that they passed out before!

TWENTY-ONE

Gribley had found a taxi already and was waiting outside. Fintan climbed in too and, much to his surprise, recognized the driver: it was Mr Rottervich!

"Oh, hello," said Fintan cheerily from the back seat. "Fancy meeting you here! I didn't know you were a taxi driver!"

He wasn't. But he had just stolen a taxi. For the last few hours he had been watching Fintan through his binoculars and getting increasingly angry. He had watched Fang's shark-toothed henchman pick the boy up from his hotel and chauffeur him to the restaurant. He'd seen the speeches and the toasts. He'd even seen the boy being presented with the silk tassel of the "Knot of Blood"!

Rottervich looked back at his passengers without smiling then sped away into the evening traffic. It was time to teach the boy a serious lesson.

"Another of your new 'friends' from the train journey, sir?" enquired Gribley.

They seemed to be popping up everywhere. Fintan was amazed at his butler's powers of deduction.

"How did you guess, Gribs?" he said. "Yes, he's a Russian businessman I met on the train!"

He leaned forwards between the front seats. "Are you feeling a bit better now, Mr Rottervich? Got over your travel sickness, yet?"

Rottervich certainly didn't look any healthier. In fact he looked a lot worse. He had managed to escape from the police station by squeezing through a tiny toilet window. It had left him covered in bruises from head to toe. He had then dropped ten metres on to the concrete below, dislocating his shoulder and giving himself a big purple bump on the forehead. As if this wasn't bad enough, his stomach was still rumbling like an angry volcano, too.

Rottervich's face darkened as if he didn't want

to talk about it. He just wanted to take Fintan somewhere secluded and get his revenge. They drove on for a while in silence until the car zoomed right past their hotel.

"Wait, stop!" said Fintan urgently. "You just missed it!"

He reached through to the front again, pointing wildly, and accidentally poked Rottervich in the eye. Luckily it was his glass one. Unluckily it fell out and began rolling around in the taxi's footwell. Fintan was hugely embarrassed and began apologizing profusely.

"Leave it!" shouted Rottervich as Fintan clambered into the front passenger seat and began ferreting around by the driver's feet.

"It's OK, I can get it," insisted Fintan, grabbing the man's left shoe. "Can you just lift your foot up, please? It's gone under one of the pedals."

The eye was a bit slippery and felt like a half-sucked gobstopper but eventually he managed to grab it.

"Got it!" he announced proudly and abruptly sat up, headbutting the one-eyed man in the face.

Rottervich, who was in enough pain already,

screamed and slammed on the brakes. The car skidded to a juddering halt, inflating the driver's airbag and pinning Rottervich back in his seat. He let out a strangulated moan.

"Really sorry about that," said Fintan, wiping the fluff from the glass eye and handing it back. "I can be a bit clumsy sometimes."

He opened the car door and got out.

"Oh, and thanks for the lift by the way. We don't mind walking from here, do we, Gribs?"

Minutes later a very angry-looking Boris Rottervich staggered into the lobby of Fintan's hotel. He was nursing a black eye, walking with a limp and had a messy nose bleed.

"Where is the boy who just came in?" he demanded. "Which room is he in?"

The woman behind the reception desk looked horrified and said nothing. She wasn't supposed to give out information like that, especially not to people who looked like crazed murderers. Rottervich decided he'd better make up a story.

"I am a taxi driver. The boy left his, er . . . his wallet in my taxi."

He took out his own wallet and waved it in the air.

The receptionist fell for the lie. "Oh, I see," she said. "In that case, he is in room number eight. Very lucky number!"

"Very *lucky*, yes," said Rottervich darkly and gripped the gun in his coat pocket.

He made his way to room eight and put his ear to the door. There were two voices coming from inside. One was definitely the annoying boy and the other was the well-dressed older man. Presumably his bodyguard.

Rottervich screwed the silencer on to his gun, knocked at the door and waited. Whoever answered the door was in for a nasty surprise. It didn't matter whether it was the boy or his bodyguard. They both had to go.

Unfortunately, so did Rottervich. A sudden revolting gurgling noise vibrated through his trousers and the contents of his stomach churned like a washing machine. The curse of the Fedora Fancies wasn't quite over. Not only did he have to go but he had to go *right away*!

When Fintan opened the door there was no one there.

"Hello?" he said, peering up and down the empty corridor. "Hello-oo?"

He gave up and went back into his room.

"That was odd," he said to Gribley. "No one there!"

TWENTY-TWO

Fang woke up feeling like she had been run over by a bus. Several of them, in fact, and they were all double-deckers. She realized she was lying in a hospital bed and had plastic tubes sticking out of her arm and her nose. Her skin had gone an unpleasant shade of grey and some of her hair had fallen out. It was quite an achievement but she looked even worse than usual. She tried sitting up but discovered her wrist was handcuffed to the bed frame.

"What happened? Where am I?" she croaked to a nearby nurse.

The nurse ignored her question and walked across to the door. "The ugly woman is awake, Inspector," she shouted to someone along the corridor.

Fang frowned. There was no need for rudeness! Moments later four policemen hurried in and gathered around her bed. They still couldn't believe their luck. Thirteen senior members of the Knot of Blood all found unconscious in a restaurant and all wearing their red tassels to prove who they were! It had been the easiest arrest ever! Even easier than the Russians they found pooping in the bushes.

"You are in hospital, Madam Fang," said the inspector. "And you are under arrest."

Under arrest? she thought with some disbelief. But the police had never managed to arrest her before. What could suddenly have gone so badly wrong? The last thing she could remember was drinking a toast to the English boy. Then a very hazy picture formed in her mind. She saw all her men collapsing around her . . . and on the table was the bottle of poisoned wine intended for Rottervich. And it was empty! Fang felt a surge of anger run through her aching body and she tugged furiously at her handcuffs.

"Fintan!" she snarled through horrible gritted teeth.

"Now you tell us everything," said the police inspector opening his notebook. "Tell us the name of your gang boss. Who is the big leader of the Knot of Blood?"

Fang was so upset she didn't even notice she had been asked a question.

"FINTAN!" she said again, much louder this time and with even more bitterness.

The policemen exchanged looks of surprise. They hadn't actually expected her to tell them anything. Especially not the name of her boss and especially not so easily!

"Did she say Fin Tan?" said the second policeman.

The others nodded. They had all heard it.

"But . . . Fin Tan's a well-respected businessman, isn't he?" said the third one. "He runs that big power station down in Mang Kee."

"A very respectable man!" added the fourth. "At least, that's what he pretends to be!"

A few more policemen came over to see what all the fuss was about.

"This is excellent!" explained the inspector. "At last we have a name! Who would have guessed that the Knot of Blood's leader was Fin Tan!"

Suddenly Fang heard her boss's name being mentioned and became aware of what was happening.

"What?" she shrieked. "How did you know that? Who told you?"

The assembled policemen stared down at her as if she was mad.

"*You* did," they said.

TWENTY-THREE

"Boss!" shouted one of Fin Tan's men, running breathlessly into the room. "We're in big trouble. Madam Fang is on TV. She's been arrested."

Fin Tan almost leapt out of his chair but was far too fat and lazy to move. "What?" he snapped, spitting out one of his cigarettes in shock.

The man changed channels and pointed urgently at the screen. "See!"

Fin Tan hurriedly put on a pair of really thick glasses that shrunk his eyes to little piggy dots. It was true. A very unwell-looking Madam Fang was being shown on the news. She was handcuffed to a hospital bed and surrounded by policemen. The reporter was explaining that she had been found unconscious in a restaurant, along with a dozen other wanted gangsters, and they had probably been poisoned.

"No!" yelled a furious Fin Tan, his face wobbling like a jelly.

This was terrible. Almost his entire gang were under arrest and, according to the TV reporter, some of them were so ill that they might not even survive. But there was even worse news to follow. The reporter said that the police now knew everything about the gang. They knew the gang boss's name and even where he was hiding. It was only a matter of time before they came to arrest him, too! The Knot of Blood was finished!

Fin Tan's little piggy eyes scowled at the television and his face flushed an angry pink.

"Who did this?" he yelled. "I want to know who is responsible!"

The news report cut to the restaurant where the mass poisoning had taken place. One of the waiters was being interviewed about what he had seen.

"It was terrible!" he sobbed, sounding very distressed. "They all just collapsed without warning so I called an ambulance straight away. It was just after the young English boy and his father had left."

"What young English boy was this?" asked the reporter.

The waiter thought for a moment. "I think he was their guest of honour. They were calling him Fintan or something."

This came as such a shock to Fin Tan that his other cigarette fell out of his mouth, too. Surely the boy couldn't have done it? The boy they had just made an honorary gang member? It didn't seem possible that the most feared gang in all of China could have been wiped out by a child!

He let out an anguished yell and threw a heavy ashtray at the TV, smashing a hole in the screen.

"Bring this interfering boy to me!" he bellowed. "And bring him to me alive! Tell whatever's left of the gang to get out there right now and find him."

TWENTY-FOUR

Boris "Dead-Eye" Rottervich had revenge on his mind, too. He had spent half the night in the toilet and the other half in his stolen taxi staring at Fintan's hotel. He knew the boy had to come out sooner or later and when he did he would squash him like a bug!

Just after nine in the morning his patience was finally rewarded as Fintan and Gribley emerged loaded with backpacks which they piled on to a little moped. They appeared to be going on a trip. Rottervich started his engine and eyed them nastily.

Unaware that he was being watched, Fintan climbed excitedly on to the bike behind Gribley. They were off to Len Ding library to see the original manuscript of *The Song of the Moon Dragon*. Fintan was excited and feeling totally confident he would find the hidden clue. However Gribley, who had trusted the boy with reading the map, wasn't even confident they would find the library. After a lot of wobbling about they finally headed out on to the main road.

Seeing his chance, Rottervich stamped down hard on his accelerator pedal and roared forwards. Unfortunately for him, so did a scruffy blue van which had been waiting around the corner. He crunched right into it and stopped dead. The driver of the blue van didn't even pause to inspect the damage but zoomed off in hot pursuit of the little moped.

Rottervich was furious. It appeared he wasn't the only one chasing the boy!

Seconds later the blue van caught up with Gribley and pulled alongside blasting its horn aggressively. The driver lowered his window, pointed at Fintan and shouted something in Chinese. He didn't sound friendly.

"That's a bit rude, isn't it, Gribs?" tutted Fintan.

"Ignore him, sir," advised Gribley.

Unfortunately, the man was now leaning out of his window and trying to grab Fintan by the sleeve. He was going to be hard to ignore. Gribley decided it might be wise to take a different route.

"Perhaps the side streets will be a little quieter, sir," he said, steering the moped sharply to the left.

The side street actually turned out to be quite busy. It was clustered with bicycles, people pulling wooden carts, and open-air cafes selling fried insects on sticks. Beeping the moped's little horn, Gribley threaded his way through the teeming crowd, trying not to bump into anyone. The van driver wasn't so fussy. He roared into the street behind them scattering tables, chairs and terrified cyclists. The air was suddenly filled with the sound of breaking glass and the screams of customers who had found bits of bicycle in their breakfasts.

Gribley hurried on until he spotted a stall selling brightly coloured clothes. He hit the brakes and swerved the moped behind a rail of silk dresses. Hopefully it would make a good hiding place.

"Awfully sorry. *Dui bu qi*, everyone," he said to a handful of shocked customers.

It was one of the useful Chinese phrases he had learnt from his book.

"I think it's gone, Gribs," said Fintan as the van smashed on past them.

But it hadn't. There was a loud screech of brakes followed by the sound of reversing. It was coming back. Gribley turned the moped around and accelerated across the street towards a narrow alley. It wouldn't be able to follow them there.

"Duck your head, sir," he yelled as they sped beneath the striped umbrellas of noodle-sellers' carts.

The van reversed right at them, crashing mindlessly through the food stalls. There was a whoosh of flames and a loud sizzling noise as several woks full of hot noodles were launched into the air. Seconds later it was followed by a thunderous crunch as the van hit a concrete wall.

"Well he's definitely gone now!" hollered Fintan, glancing back over his shoulder.

The man had been pulled from his van and was being attacked by several furious stall holders. All of them were coated in sticky noodles and dumplings.

They tore on down the alley but the way ahead

was blocked. An angry man on a motorbike was coming towards them, screaming threats at the top of his voice. They were trapped. Gribley skidded sideways and turned into an open doorway, desperately hoping it wasn't a dead end. It was someone's house! A wrinkly-faced old lady was standing at her stove stirring something in a pot. She looked understandably surprised to see two strangers on a moped ride into her house.

"Awfully sorry!" shouted Gribley as he steered through her kitchen and out of the back door.

The man on the motorbike crashed in behind them, still yelling terrible things in Chinese.

This was too much for the old lady, who whacked him in the face with a frying pan. Having one vehicle in her house was bad enough but she wasn't putting up with two!

"Master Fintan, sir," said Gribley as they emerged into an even narrower alley. "There appear to be people who are rather angry with us. Might you have upset anyone recently?"

"Don't think so, Gribs," said Fintan, trying to remember some of his recent disasters.

Maybe they were staff from the hotel where he

had accidentally knocked over a potted plant in the reception. If so it was a bit of an overreaction! Then again he had also broken the sink, made a hole in the wardrobe and set fire to his pillow. But that was all. Nothing serious!

"Maybe they're just bad drivers or something?"

Gribley doubted this. He knew from experience that when complete strangers started trying to kill them it was usually something to do with the boy.

As soon as they were back on the road, another motorbike, a scooter and a heavy truck all thundered up behind them. Right at the back of the group was a very unwell-looking Rottervich in his battered taxi. It had a huge dent in the side and black smoke was belching from the engine. Something even worse was belching from his upset stomach.

"Brace yourself, sir," announced Gribley, steering the moped through a gap in a wooden fence. "This may be a little bumpy."

They found themselves in a construction site where dozens of workers were building a bridge over the river. It was a mess of mud, heavy machinery and bamboo scaffolding. Gribley sped across the lumpy ground hoping to lose their pursuers in the maze of building equipment. Seconds later the huge truck smashed in behind them followed by the others.

Almost immediately the little scooter sunk up to its axles in gloopy mud and fell spectacularly apart. Rottervich's taxi ploughed into the back of it, flipped on to its roof and skidded to a halt. For a moment Rottervich hung upside down, suspended by his seat belt, and shouted some terrible Russian swear words. Then gravity started doing strange things to his stomach. Hurriedly he scrambled from the wreckage and limped desperately to the building site's only toilet. It was one of those portable blue plastic ones that smelt appalling but he was in no condition to be choosy. He scrambled inside and locked the door.

The enormous lorry, meanwhile, was gaining on the little moped. Gribley turned sharply to the left and headed towards the river. With any luck they could escape over the half-finished bridge. He splashed through a swampy mess of puddles, sending up a thick brown spray from his back wheel which splattered all over the windscreen of the lorry behind. The driver couldn't see where he was going. In panic he turned on his wipers but they just smeared the mud about and made things even worse. With a horrendous thud he crashed into a heavily loaded dumper truck, tipping it on to its side. Several tons of concrete pipes cascaded to the ground and tumbled in all directions.

Fintan looked back and saw something emerge from the cloud of dust and falling debris.

"The lorry's stopped, Gribs!" he announced happily. "But the motorbike's still after us."

It was a big, black monster of a machine which looked powerful enough to crush them. And it was going really fast. Gribley squeezed the bike between two enormous bulldozers and headed for the half-built bridge. The black bike followed, scraping through the narrow gap in a shower of metallic sparks.

"I have no intention of stopping, sir," said Gribley as a group of worried-looking men in hard hats frantically waved their arms at him.

He swerved around them and steered up a ramp on to the bridge. It was nowhere near finished. In places it was nothing more than bare steel girders, no wider than the moped's wheels, but he kept going.

So did the black bike. It roared up dangerously close behind them while the turbulent brown river rushed by fifteen metres below. Fintan closed his eyes and held his breath.

Meanwhile, back in the building site one of the massive concrete pipes had reached the muddy slope of the river bank. It rolled lumpily downhill until it thumped into the portable plastic toilet. There was a hollow thud and a muffled scream. The toilet wobbled from side to side then fell into the river.

When Fintan opened his eyes they were safely on the other side of the river but the motorbike was still right on their tail.

"Perhaps we can hide in here, sir," announced Gribley, abruptly turning off the road and into a busy car park.

According to a large sign they were at the entrance to the Great Wall of China.

"Cool!" said Fintan.

The place was packed. Hundreds of tourists were queuing for tickets and flocking around souvenir stalls. Gribley threaded his way through them apologizing for being a nuisance. They were never going to outrun the powerful bike so their only chance was to disappear somewhere in the crowd. Unfortunately the biker was refusing to be shaken off. He followed right behind them, smashing through the souvenir stalls in a storm of broken plastic. The crowd scattered, screaming in terror, while Gribley hurriedly looked around for a way out. Their only option was the entrance to the Great Wall itself.

"Shouldn't we get tickets?" asked Fintan as they headed to the front of the queue.

Gribley was embarrassed to admit it but it looked like they were going to have to break the rules.

"Ordinarily yes, sir," he said. "But I'm afraid these are not ordinary circumstances. This is something of an emergency."

He beeped the moped's little horn, frightening a cluster of tourists out of the way, and steered right on to the Great Wall of China!

The Great Wall made a surprisingly good road; it was a smooth stone walkway about three metres wide with low battlements on either side. It snaked its way over hills and down valleys like an ancient roller coaster. Their poor little moped juddered and shook up the stone steps but somehow kept going. Every few hundred metres they passed through one of the Wall's many watchtowers but there was nowhere to hide and no way to get off. They had no choice but to keep going. Behind them the monstrous bike was now so close that Fintan could almost smell the rider's breath.

Beyond the next watchtower they were confronted by a serious obstacle. Right in front of them was a large parade of people banging drums, clashing cymbals together and waving flags. Others were leaping and dancing beneath a huge, brightly coloured dragon costume. There was no way through.

"What'll we do, Gribs?" yelled a terrified Fintan.

Gribley had to think fast. "I suggest we hold on tightly, sir."

With surprising precision he steered the little moped straight up the dragon's tail and launched the bike into the air. They sailed high over its head, cleared the whole parade and made a perfect landing on the other side.

The black motorbike, however, steamed right into it. There was a sudden frenzy of screaming people, ripping flags and flying drums. The bike zoomed on through the crowd, snatching the costume right off the dancers' backs. Seconds later Fintan and Gribley watched in bewilderment as they were overtaken by a ten-metre long, goggle-eyed dragon doing about one hundred kilometres an hour. It zigzagged blindly from side to side, thrashing its tail, then hit the battlements and shot over the edge of the wall. With its wide mouth flapping, it flew through the air and disappeared noisily into the trees below.

"That was brilliant, Gribs!" shouted an elated Fintan. "I didn't know you could do stuff like that!"

Gribley smiled modestly. There was a lot Fintan didn't know about him.

"Now, sir, we should probably go back and purchase our entry tickets."

Luckily the rest of their journey was a lot easier. They didn't get lost much and Fintan only dropped the map once and fell off the bike twice so, all in all, it was pretty uneventful. After four hours of bumping along narrow dirt tracks they finally reached their destination: the little town of Len Ding.

"We have arrived, sir," announced Gribley as they climbed painfully off the bike and leant it against a wall.

Their poor, battered moped didn't look very well. Its engine had been coughing like a sick seal and several bits had fallen off.

"Good," said Fintan, stretching himself. "My bum was really starting to ache!"

Len Ding turned out to be a very beautiful, very old and surprisingly busy town. It was a maze of narrow streets lined with ancient dark wooden houses and bustling with hundreds of people. The air smelt of woodsmoke, incense and exotic food.

The old library, when they found it, was fabulous too. A traditional brightly painted building with a broad curving roof. The inside was, of course, full of books. Lots of them. Fintan had never seen so many books. Many looked and smelt ancient. Gribley breathed in the atmosphere and smiled. This was his kind of place!

Sitting silently reading a book was an incredibly fragile-looking old man with a deeply lined, leathery face ending in a wispy white beard. He was presumably the librarian.

"*Nee how*," said Gribley, opening his phrase book. "*Nee kay bang wo ma?*" which he hoped meant *hello can you help me?*

The old man continued reading. He looked almost as ancient as some of the books.

"Maybe he's a bit deaf?" whispered Fintan. "Or stuffed or something?"

Gribley tried again as loudly as he thought decent in a public library.

"*Nee kay bang wo ma?*" he repeated.

The librarian looked up. He still didn't seem to understand but at least it proved he wasn't stuffed.

"D'you want me to have a go, Gribs?" asked Fintan. "Maybe your pronunciation isn't very good."

Gribley frowned. There was nothing wrong with his pronunciation.

"Why don't you just tell him we're looking for the lost village of Yin?" continued Fintan.

The elderly librarian's face lit up. "Yin?" he said, suddenly looking interested. "You want to find Yin?"

He put on a different pair of glasses and studied the odd pair standing in front of him. A refined-looking Englishman in a dark suit and a scruffy-haired boy wearing shorts that were too big for him. They didn't look like the usual adventurers that passed through.

"So . . . you're looking for the hidden clue, are you?" he said, sounding as if he had been through this many times before. "No one's ever found it, you know."

Gribley nodded meekly and tried to look modest and humble.

"Ah, but I bet we will!" grinned Fintan, giving a double thumbs-up. "We're proper explorers, we are!"

The old librarian sighed, hauled himself upright and began shuffling away.

"Follow me then. The book's this way."

Fintan and Gribley followed him down a flight of wooden stairs into a cavernous basement. It smelt damp and centuries old. In the furthest, darkest corner they came to a black door decorated with strange symbols. The librarian unlocked it and ushered them into a tiny room.

"It's in here," he said, switching on a hopelessly dim light. "You will be careful, of course? The manuscript is extremely valuable."

"Of course," promised Gribley, painfully aware that he was accompanied by the world's most accident-prone boy.

The old librarian nodded and left them to it. In the centre of the room stood a carved wooden podium and resting on it was a stack of very fragile yellow paper.

"Is that it then?" asked Fintan, peering quizzically at it. He had no idea what a manuscript was supposed to look like. "Wow. The pages aren't even stapled together!"

He had no idea what a manuscript was supposed to look like. Gribley nodded in respectful silence. He was standing in the presence of the actual, original handwritten manuscript of *The Song of the Moon Dragon*. It was all very overwhelming.

"Right then," announced Fintan, gleefully rubbing his hands together. "Let's start looking for that hidden clue, shall we?"

He strode over to the manuscript and stared at it thoughtfully. It was covered in Chinese writing.

"Hmm, hidden clue, hidden clue. . ." he muttered to himself, stroking his chin and tilting his head sideways in case it might help. "So . . . what exactly are we looking for, Gribs?"

Gribley sighed. "No one knows, sir. It's possible there's no clue in there at all."

"'Course there is!" laughed Fintan, casually holding a page up to his eyes and squinting at it. "There's always a clue! And we're going to find it!"

Gribley stepped forward. He couldn't help feeling that a terrible accident was only seconds away.

"Perhaps it would be best if you allowed me to look, sir?" he suggested, gently taking the priceless page out of Fintan's grubby hands.

Fintan had to agree. Gribley knew far more about this sort of thing than he did: poetry, ancient manuscripts and the like. Not to mention the fact that he was pretty good at reading Chinese. Gribley was also far less likely to rip it, drop it or spill his drink on it.

"That's a very good point, Gribs," he said. "Probably best if you look first."

He went and sat on a long wooden bench by the wall.

For the next hour and a half Fintan sat and waited while Gribley worked his way through the fragile pages. There was nothing unusual there at all.

Just page after page of beautifully written Chinese characters. Nothing scribbled in the margins. No strange codes or secret messages. No curious symbols or backwards writing. He tried reading it sideways and upwards and at an angle. Nothing.

"Take your time, Gribs!" said Fintan, even though he was itching to get up and help.

Gribley wondered whether the clue had been split into pieces and was spread across many pages? He carried the manuscript to another long wooden bench and carefully counted the pages into six equal piles along it. He read the first word of each pile but that didn't work. He tried reading the last word and the middle word but it still made no sense. He then arranged the pages in groups of seven and eight and nine and tried again. Gibberish.

After two hours Fintan was getting very fidgety.

"How's it going, Gribs?" he asked, strolling over to have a look.

"Slowly I'm afraid, sir," sighed Gribley. "The number of possible combinations is almost infinite."

Fintan nodded wisely, as if he understood what this meant, and sat down on the very end of Gribley's bench. It tipped up like a seesaw, catapulting the entire manuscript across the room. Priceless sheets of parchment flew through the air and fluttered to the floor like falling leaves.

"Sorry!" blurted Fintan, leaping up in an embarrassed hurry and gathering the sheets back together.

"For goodness sake be careful with those, sir!" begged Gribley, horrified at the boy's clumsiness. "Please let me do it."

He bent down and began delicately picking up the rest of the scattered manuscript while Fintan backed out of the way.

"We must be very careful not to get them out of order," continued Gribley.

Fintan hadn't thought of that. Chinese writing looked the same to him either way up so he hadn't being paying much attention.

"Sorry," he said again.

It was a hopeless mess. He stared at the handful of pages he was clutching. They had been shuffled, turned back to front and upside down. Then he noticed something odd; a vague shape. He held the pages up to the weak lamp so that he could see it more clearly.

"Ha! Look at that, Gribs," he said. "It makes a sort of picture."

It was true. Where the light shone through the overlapping Chinese characters there was a distinct, dark image of a creature holding a curved sword. It looked like a sort of winged snake with long whiskers and horns.

"Good Lord. . ." breathed Gribley, his mouth hanging open in astonishment. "It's the Moon Dragon!"

"Is it?" enquired Fintan, staring hard at it as if he ought to recognize it.

Gribley was stunned. There had been a clue in the manuscript after all! And Fintan Fedora, the walking disaster of a boy, had accidentally found it.

TWNETY-FIVE

That evening they booked themselves into a scruffy little guest house feeling exhausted. The room had two lumpy beds, a creaky old fan and a wash bowl full of cold water.

"I still don't get it though, Gribs," mused Fintan, lying in his uncomfortable bed, unable to sleep. "The picture of the dragon with the sword. What does it mean?"

Gribley, who had tucked himself neatly into the other bed, was already pondering the matter.

"An interesting question, sir," he said. "Luckily I am familiar with this particular creature. It is the famous Moon Dragon from the Master's unfinished book. He painted it many times and sculpted many different versions of it during his lifetime. However, there is only one place where it is shown holding a curved sword . . . and that is at the Temple of The Sky."

Fintan was constantly amazed at how much his butler knew about things. It must be because he read books.

"Cool!" he said, sitting up in bed. "So is that where the lost village is then?"

Gribley shook his head.

"Unlikely, sir. The Temple of the Sky is in a dry, mountainous region, whereas Yin was supposed to be in a lush valley by a river. I believe the dragon may just be pointing us to the location of a second clue."

"A second clue?" said Fintan brightly. "Brilliant! It's like a treasure hunt or something. So where is this Temple of the Sky?"

"Not terribly far, sir. I shall show you on the map in the mor—"

Before Gribley could finish his sentence a deafening barrage of noise shook the room and shocked them both out of bed. It sounded like hundreds of people were firing guns at each other outside. They peeked nervously out through the frayed curtains into the dark street where billows of smoke were filling the air and bright flashes were illuminating an excited crowd.

"It's just firecrackers, sir," said Gribley, relieved that it wasn't more people trying to kill them. They'd had enough excitement for one day. "It must be some sort of local festival."

"Cool!" said Fintan.

He liked the noisy way these Chinese people did things. Fintan and Gribley stood at the window together and watched until the festivities died down, then settled back into their lumpy beds and went to sleep.

TWENTY-SIX

According to the map it was only eighty kilometres to the Temple of the Sky which meant they could be there in just over an hour. Unless of course someone tried to run them over again. They piled their bags on to the moped and prepared to climb aboard. Unfortunately the poor battered machine had had enough. It let out one last painful creak and collapsed. Both its wheels fell off and the engine dropped out. Fintan stared at it sadly.

"Don't suppose you brought a spanner, did you, Gribs?" he said hopefully.

It was an unfortunate setback. They were going to have to walk to the temple now. With heavy hearts and even heavier rucksacks they set off into the forest. Suddenly eighty kilometres sounded like a very long way. It was going to take at least two days and it wasn't going to be easy either. The air was muggy and filled with annoying insects, while the terrain felt like it was constantly going uphill. On the plus side though, the forest was stunningly beautiful. A tangle of emerald green foliage with a surprising number of weird, wild creatures living in it.

"Do you think we'll see any pandas, Gribs?" asked Fintan after watching a pair of strange blue-faced monkeys saunter by.

"I shouldn't think so, sir," said Gribley. "There are very few areas of giant panda habitat left. And this isn't one of them."

"Shame," said Fintan. "I've always wanted a panda. I bet I'd be the only kid in school with a pet one."

"Indeed you would, sir, but even if we did find one, I'm afraid you wouldn't be allowed to take it home. Giant pandas are extremely rare and protected animals. And besides, where would you get the bamboo to feed it?"

Fintan shrugged his shoulders, not seeing this as a major problem. "I dunno," he said. "Pet shop?"

The look on Gribley's face suggested this wasn't the right answer. They pushed on deeper into the forest, crunching through a carpet of pine needles and fallen leaves. Other than the occasional encounter with a fragile-looking spotted deer and Fintan tripping over his bootlaces, nothing much happened. But after the boy had fallen flat on his face for the third time Gribley finally persuaded him to do his boots up properly.

As Fintan was kneeling down tying his laces, a small red and black stripy snake crawled across his boot. He had never seen such a brightly coloured one before and instantly took a liking to it. If Gribley wouldn't let him have a pet panda, then maybe he'd have to make do with a snake. He watched it slither silently through the leaf litter and wondered what would be a good name for a pet snake. He decided not to tell Gribley about it just in case he came up with some silly objection.

"Come on, Stripy Steve," he whispered, opening his rucksack and gently persuading the highly venomous snake inside. "There's a good boy!"

*

Eventually Fintan and Gribley emerged from the forest and found themselves on a narrow dirt road. Gribley consulted the compass and suggested they follow the road southwards.

With Stripy Steve happily asleep in Fintan's rucksack they trudged along the road for about an hour until they heard a weird noise. Something was coming. A rattling old van, which looked like it was held together with rust, slowed down and stopped for them.

"Hello, persons!" grinned the van driver, displaying his three remaining teeth. "Very nice happy and sunshine! How am I? You want lifting?"

Fintan liked the man immediately.

"Hello," said Gribley. "Are you going anywhere near the Temple of the Sky?"

"Yeee-es!" beamed the man, opening his passenger door for them. "Also no. Please getting in, OK?"

"Very kind of you," said Gribley as they climbed gratefully into the van.

They drove off down the bumpy road at a slow but steady pace. It felt good to be giving their aching feet a rest.

"Today I am going Mang Kee!" announced the van driver proudly.

Fintan had to smother a giggle. The man looked like he had been going manky for some time.

"Many cigarettes today," he went on, gesturing to the back of his van which was stacked to the roof with thousands of boxes of them. "Very important delivery in Mang Kee, oh yes!"

Fintan and Gribley nodded and pretended to be impressed.

"I am today being Mister Pong," shouted the driver over the rattling noise of the engine.

Fintan tried hard not to snigger again. It was everyone else who had funny names, not him! First it had been Dong, then Fang, and now Mister Pong! They *had* to be doing it on purpose.

"Mr Gribley and Master Fintan," said Gribley.

Mr Pong looked stunned for a moment. Then his face spread into a huge gummy grin.

"Fin Tan?" he blurted, barely able to speak through hysterical laughter. "Fin Tan! Ha ha ha!"

Gribley looked thoroughly confused while Fintan folded his arms and frowned. This joke about his name was wearing a bit thin.

"It's not that funny," he said.

"Oh dear. Fin Tan very skinny," guffawed Mr. Pong. "Also big fatty. Very funny!"

In fact it was funny enough to keep Mr Pong amused for several more kilometres. He was still chortling to himself as the van began rattling along the shore of a massive lake. It was so big that they could barely see the other side. Here and there the water was studded with towering pillars of rock draped in rich greenery which looked like weird, alien islands in an endless sea.

"Is this the seaside?" asked Fintan, squinting into the distance.

Gribley consulted his map. "No, sir. I believe it's actually an artificial lake for the region's hydro power station. It was created when they built a dam across the valley."

"Very big lake today," agreed the driver, pointing and nodding.

Meanwhile, down in Fintan's rucksack, Stripy Steve had woken up and was crawling out to explore his new surroundings. The floor of the van was full of interesting smells and bits of dropped food but there were far too many pairs of boots down there for his liking. He preferred warm, dark places. Which is why he slithered up Mr Pong's trouser leg. Normally Mr Pong was a very good and safe driver. He had been making deliveries to Mang Kee for over twenty years without a single accident. However, today was the first time he had ever given a lift to Fintan Fedora and also the first time he had tried driving with a venomous snake in his trousers.

"Oh crikey!" he shouted, letting go of the steering wheel and flapping his trouser legs about. "Oh crikey goodness!"

The van jerked sharply sideways, left the road and thundered up a grassy slope. Gribley was thrown against the windscreen while Fintan found himself being tossed helplessly around with several large boxes of cigarettes. For a moment everything was a blur of shrieking and tumbling as they jolted blindly out of control. Then Gribley saw a vast expanse of water looming up in front of them. They were heading straight for the lake! He stretched his leg across Mr Pong's struggling body and stamped down hard on the brake. The van rattled to a halt in a cloud of dust with its front wheels teetering over the edge of the lake.

"Oh dear, very bad today!" yelled Mr Pong, wriggling and shrieking like a terrified schoolgirl.

He yanked open his door and leapt out. There was an ominous creak as the van tipped a little further towards the water. Fintan was lying upside down with his head in the footwell and his feet in the air.

"Are you all right, Gribs?" he said.

"Very well, thank you, sir," said Gribley, with his foot still planted on the brake pedal. "Although I think it might be wise for us to leave the vehicle."

Fintan didn't need much persuading. Very gently he opened the passenger door and crawled out. Gribley followed close behind, dragging their bags. Almost immediately the van toppled over the edge and plunged down into the lake.

Mr Pong stopped jumping around and stared as his precious van disappeared from view in a violent surge of bubbles. Moments later several thousand packets of soggy cigarettes floated to the surface. Just to make things even worse, Stripy Steve wriggled up his thigh and hid in Mr Pong's underpants. He screamed, gave his trousers a final desperate shake, then took a flying leap into the lake.

*

"Shame about Mr Pong wasn't it," said Fintan as they trudged down the dusty road.

It had been an hour since they left the poor man thrashing around in the water. He had been absolutely inconsolable and refused all their offers of help.

"Wonder why he went all funny like that?"

Gribley raised an eyebrow but said nothing. People didn't leap around and jump into lakes for no reason. He suspected it might have had something to do with the boy but he had no idea what.

The track gradually led them away from the lake shore and into a conifer forest. And it was all uphill again.

"Only a few more miles now, sir," said Gribley, trying to sound encouraging.

"Good," breathed Fintan. "I'm worn out!"

They trudged on until the failing light made it impossible to continue, then dropped their bags and pitched their tent beneath the trees.

It was the first time either of them had ever camped out in the Chinese wilderness so the bizarre night-time noises came as a bit of a surprise. Unseen creatures creaked like rusty wheels, whistled, chimed and grunted in the darkness. At one point something large snuffled around their tent before peeing all over it.

"D'you know what I don't understand, Gribs?" said Fintan from his sleeping bag.

"Could you be a little more specific perhaps, sir?" said Gribley.

There were probably hundreds of things the boy didn't understand.

"This poet bloke . . ." continued Fintan, "this Great Master of Yin . . . why did he bother leaving all those clues and stuff? Why was it all such a big secret?"

"A most interesting question, sir," said Gribley, pleased that they weren't discussing the lack of peanut butter in China again. "Eight hundred years ago he wrote a poem called *The Tyrant*. It was about a fierce warlord who ruled over the region in those days. The poem is supposed to have angered the warlord so much that he ordered his men to go to the poet's house and kill him."

Fintan found this hard to believe. "Kill him? Because of a poem?" he gasped.

"Indeed, sir. The warlord was a notoriously

unpleasant ruler. So the Great Master, fearing for his life, abandoned his writing and went into hiding."

"Don't blame him," said Fintan, nodding wisely in the dark.

"Though before disappearing he is meant to have left certain clues for his supporters to follow, such as the image of the dragon in the manuscript. According to the legend, the village was finally discovered by the warlord's soldiers and destroyed. The poet was never seen again and his last poem was left unfinished."

Fintan thought about this in silence for a while. It was quite an epic story.

"So . . . in all this time no one's ever found the village of Yin?" he said.

"Indeed," agreed Gribley.

"And we're the first people ever to find the clue to where it is?"

Gribley nodded.

"Cool!" said Fintan.

He had no idea ancient Chinese poetry could be so exciting.

TWENTY-SEVEN

Dawn came ridiculously early and brought with it the smell of moss and damp pine trees which was a lot better than the smell of the tent. Gribley made a simple breakfast of rice porridge while Fintan repacked his rucksack. It appeared Stripy Steve had escaped back into the wild already, which was a bit disappointing.

"How much further is it?" asked Fintan as he shook the bugs out of his sleeping bag.

Gribley checked the map and surveyed the local area.

"Not far at all, sir," he announced. "In fact we're almost there."

Fintan looked around. There were conifer trees, rocks and moss.

"Are we?" he said. "Where's the temple then?"

Gribley pointed upwards. For some reason the Temple of the Sky had been built at the top of a mountain. Fintan squinted up through the trees and saw an ancient pagoda-shaped building clinging to the bare rock.

"That's a daft place to put a temple," he said.

They donned their backpacks and began climbing the steep mountain path. The stone steps were centuries old and had been worn smooth by thousands of feet. In places they had crumbled completely away. Several times Gribley had to help Fintan across a terrifying gap, sending loose rocks cascading hundreds of metres down the mountainside. One false step and they might end up tumbling down into the valley, too.

It took a whole hour to reach the top but it was well worth it. The Temple of the Sky was stunning. A red, green and gold pagoda, five storeys high, with a spire projecting from the very top. A pair of stone lions guarded the gateway and an iron cauldron stood between them, smouldering with incense. A young monk dressed in an orange robe was sweeping the steps to the entrance as they arrived.

"Look, Gribs," announced Fintan, pointing excitedly at the man. "A real monk!"

Gribley gently lowered the boy's hand. "Perhaps we should have a quick word about how to behave in temples, sir," he whispered. "There are certain rules to follow and I'm afraid pointing is considered rather rude."

"Oh, sorry," said Fintan, who had been hoping to create a good impression for a change.

"Generally, one should behave respectfully in a temple," continued Gribley. "When greeting a monk, place your hands together like this and make a little bow."

He demonstrated what he meant and Fintan attempted to copy. He looked like a large, awkward praying mantis. The monk stared at the visitors in patient silence.

"Always remove your shoes and your hat. Never touch the statues or point your feet towards them and definitely don't say anything rude."

He paused and thought about this for a moment. "Actually, it's probably best if you don't say anything at all."

Fintan nodded.

"Okey doke, Gribs," he said, dumping his hat and his backpack on the ground. "Doesn't sound too hard."

He immediately plonked one dirty boot up on a small statue's head and began undoing the laces. The monk was horrified and Gribley coughed one of his special "stop it" coughs.

"Sorry," blurted Fintan. "Forgot that bit."

He lifted his foot into the air instead and continued untying the lace while hopping about on one leg. Balancing on one leg wasn't one of Fintan's strong points. In fact neither was balancing on two. Gribley could sense trouble brewing.

"Perhaps it would be wiser to sit down to remove your shoes, sir," he suggested, while attempting to steer the boy to the ground.

"I'm OK, thanks," grunted Fintan, tugging awkwardly at his boot. "Nearly . . . got it."

The boot, as well as a revoltingly stinky sock, unglued themselves from his foot. Fintan lost his balance and fell over while his boot sailed through the air and hit the monk in the face. The sock landed in the smoking cauldron, sending up a cloud of hot ash, then burst into flames.

"Oh no, I'm really sorry!" apologized Fintan, trying to fish out the burning sock with a small stick.

As first impressions go, it could probably have gone better.

TWENTY-EIGHT

Meanwhile the horribly fat gang boss, Fin Tan, was sitting in his secret hideout pretending to be a respectable businessman. He lived far away from civilization in a remote valley called Mang Kee. It was a bit of a dump and there wasn't much there but he owned it all. He owned the power station, the massive concrete dam, and the handful of ugly little buildings that squatted in its shadow. It was a miserable, polluted, dirty, noisy place full of iron pipes and throbbing machinery but it made an excellent hiding place and the police never bothered him there.

His secret hideout took up the entire top floor of the dam and, unlike the rest of Mang Kee, was absolute luxury. He had equipped it with all the latest technology and the best furniture that money could buy. The walls were covered in ridiculously expensive art and the floors were scattered with tiger-skin rugs. He even had an indoor ornamental fountain full of champagne.

But despite being surrounded by all these luxuries Fin Tan was feeling terrible. The delivery truck hadn't turned up and he had no cigarettes! Smoking was like eating and drinking to Fin Tan. Actually, it was more like breathing. He couldn't live without it. He stared angrily at his fancy gold watch and began to sweat even more than usual. This was serious! So serious, in fact, that he heaved his fat body out of his comfy chair and took the lift down to the power station.

"Where are the cigarettes?" he wheezed at the supervisor. "Is the van here yet?"

"No sign of it. Sorry, boss," said the supervisor nervously, hoping he wasn't about to get the blame.

Fin Tan growled with frustration and stomped into the plant's enormous turbine hall. The air was hot and humid and the noise was deafening. At least twenty men in orange hard hats were working there and with luck one of them was bound to have a spare cigarette.

"Cigarette?" he shouted at the nearest workman.

The man looked terrified and shook his head. Fin Tan could feel himself getting increasingly desperate. His skin felt itchy all over and he was sweating like a garden sprinkler. Asking the workers one by one was going to take far too long so he went to the main fuse box and yanked the power switch down.

"OK, who's got a cigarette?" he yelled as the power plant fell eerily quiet.

No one spoke. All the workers stared at him from behind their machines and looked afraid. Their boss was a scary bully of a man after all. He worked them hard, paid them very little, and treated them cruelly.

"No one?" he squealed, finding it hard to believe. "Come on. Somebody's got to have one! I need a cigarette right now!"

He stood with his hands on his hips and glared at his workforce like a huge, chubby baby. Still nobody said anything. This was unbearable. Fin Tan's blood pressure rose to boiling point and one of his piggy little eyes started to twitch. He clenched his podgy fists, punched the factory supervisor in the head and stormed outside.

For a while he paced around, kicking at chunks of industrial rubbish and splashing through oily puddles. Was it really possible that there wasn't a single cigarette left in the whole of Mang Kee? What on earth had happened to the delivery truck?

At that moment he caught sight of a bedraggled, dripping wet figure shuffling towards him.

It was Mr Pong.

TWENTY-NINE

Back at the Temple of the Sky the monks had politely asked Fintan to wait outside just in case there were any more little accidents. He had reluctantly agreed it was probably a good idea, so Gribley had been taken into the temple alone. It was dark and silent inside and smelt of ancient pine wood. With the help of his phrase book Gribley asked if he could see the work of the Great Master of Yin. The young monk seemed very happy to show him. They walked through a dimly lit chamber to a large wooden doorway covered in carvings. It was spectacular. Wild animals and birds were shown frolicking among willowy trees while on either side a pair of identical young women bowed to each other.

"Carved by the Master of Yin," said the monk proudly.

Gribley was hugely impressed. It was one of the Great Master's works which he had never heard of before. A very rare thing!

"It's wonderful, thank you," breathed Gribley, getting out his phrase book again. "But I was actually hoping to see the Moon Dragon . . . er . . . *yoolang long zee*?"

The monk didn't understand him. Maybe his Chinese pronunciation wasn't that good after all. Gribley repeated the phrase and made a meandering gesture with his hand which was meant to look like the dragon's curving body.

"*Shoo-ee?*" said the young monk looking confused.

Now Gribley was confused too. That wasn't the word for dragon, was it? He flicked through his phrase book until he found it. *Shoo-ee* meant river. Maybe his hand gestures weren't that good either! He tried again with a slightly more believable dragon mime until the monk finally understood.

He led Gribley through the carved doorway into a fabulously decorated, circular room. Ahead of them sat a row of magnificent statues dressed in orange silk robes while on all sides beautiful objects glinted in the candlelight. The young monk gestured upwards. High above them the entire domed ceiling had been painted with stunning murals. Gribley gazed up in awe. There, right above him, was the Moon Dragon with its curved sword, brightly coloured and several metres long. It was a stunning sight.

The monk bowed slightly and quietly left the room. Gribley stood alone in the silence studying the dragon's long snake-like body curving sinuously across the ceiling. It really did look a lot like a river. A sudden exciting idea leapt into his mind. Perhaps it was depicting an actual river? Maybe the dragon's body was a kind of map which showed the way to the lost village! The more he looked at it the more obvious it became. Hurriedly he unfolded his map of China and searched for anything with a similar shape, turning it around in his hands and trying it from all angles. Suddenly there it was. The dragon's body was almost exactly the same shape as a remote section of the Black River. A shudder of excitement ran down his spine. Bit by bit the ancient secret was revealing itself!

THIRTY

"You! Delivery man!" shouted Fin Tan as the dripping man trudged towards him. "Where are my cigarettes?"

Mr Pong looked exhausted. He had walked all night in soaking wet clothes with water squirting out of his lace holes. He also appeared to have lost his trousers. Taking them off was the only way he could get rid of the snake.

"All gone!" he wailed sadly. "All gone to the bottom of the lake."

Fin Tan's face darkened with fury. He grabbed the poor soggy man by his lapels and lifted him off the ground.

"What do you mean?" he yelled right into his face.

"Oh crikey, it was a terrible accident," continued Mr Pong, sniffing back the tears. "My poor van went into the lake. Everything was ruined."

The fat gangster trembled with anger and went weak at the knees. "You mean . . . ALL the cigarettes are gone?" he wailed.

Mr Pong nodded. "Very sorry," he said. "But on the bright side at least nobody got hurt. I escaped OK and so did the English man and his little boy. Only the cigarettes got drowned."

"English boy? What English boy?" snapped Fin Tan.

Mr Pong managed a slight smile despite being held in the gangster's furious grip. "Oh, this will make you laugh," he said. "I gave a lift to a skinny English boy and guess what? His name was Fin Tan, too! Hilarious!"

Fin Tan didn't find it hilarious in the slightest. It hadn't been an accident at all! That horrible interfering English boy had deliberately sabotaged his essential cigarette supply! The fiend!

He roared with rage and began punching Mr Pong. It wasn't his fault but he needed to hit someone! Luckily Fin Tan's mobile rang before he could do too much harm. He dropped the soggy man to the ground and snatched up his phone, desperate to hear some good news. So far, everyone he had sent to catch the boy had been involved in a weird traffic accident. They had been ringing him from various prisons, hospitals and roadside ditches with an assortment of broken limbs. One had even lost all his teeth after an old lady hit him in the face with a frying pan.

Unfortunately it was more bad news.

"Sorry, Mr Fin Tan, sir," said a quiet, trembling voice.

It was the man from the black motorbike speaking from halfway up the tree he was stuck in, tangled up in a dragon costume.

"I nearly caught the boy on the Great Wall, sir. But he got away. And I don't know where he's gone."

"You let him get away? What is wrong with you?" yelled Fin Tan. "You are useless. All of you, absolutely useless!"

He hung up and stood there seething with rage and gave Mr Pong a swift kick. There was now just one member of his gang left: the Knot of Blood's top martial arts expert known only as the Scarlet

Whirlwind. He was a deadly kung fu master with the tracking skills of a bloodhound, the strength of a bull and the speed of a striking cobra. He was also Fin Tan's last remaining hope. If anyone could track down and capture the boy, it was the Scarlet Whirlwind!

THIRTY-ONE

Meanwhile, outside the temple, Fintan had grown bored with standing around and wandered off for a look around. He had climbed a creaky old spiral staircase and was sitting on a balcony near the very top. The view was stunning. He could see for hundreds of kilometres into the misty, mountainous distance. Rivers wound through the conifer forests, sparkling in the sunlight, while large white birds flapped effortlessly through the sky. It was all very relaxing and probably more fun than looking at some dusty old painting anyway. He delved into his bag and pulled out a soggy sandwich filled with some sort of steamed pork and drippy sauce. It was almost impossible to get a proper peanut butter sandwich in China so this weird local concoction would have to do.

Way below him on the steep, rocky path, he could just about make out someone dressed all in red making their way up. Instead of climbing slowly and carefully this person appeared to be leaping up the mountain with great ease. Fintan watched, fascinated, for some time until the man finally reached the top. He was wearing what looked like red silk pyjamas and had a bandana tied around his head. It was the Scarlet Whirlwind!

"Hello," said Fintan through a mouthful of sandwich. "That was brilliant! Are you an acrobat?"

The man jerked his gaze upwards and seemed to know who he was.

"Boy! You must come with me!" he shouted aggressively. "Mr Fin Tan wants to speak with you."

"No thank you," said Fintan.

He knew it was never a good idea to go off with weird-looking strangers, especially ones in their pyjamas.

"You come now!" demanded the Scarlet Whirlwind even louder than before.

"I'd rather not," said Fintan, hoping the man might go away.

He didn't. In fact he bared his teeth and took up a kung fu fighting position.

"Is this about his present?" asked Fintan, suddenly remembering the stacking doll being thrown out of the train window. "Because I haven't got it any more, honest!"

The man looked as if he hadn't understood a word.

"Hang on a minute, I'll look it up. . ." said Fintan, putting down his drippy sandwich and searching through his Chinese phrase book. The words for "present", "lost" and "accidentally got thrown away" weren't easy to find and even harder to pronounce, but he did his best.

"*Lee-woo*. . ." he said, rifling through the pages. "*Lee-see*. . ."

There were painfully long pauses between each word but he struggled on anyway.

"*Doo-shee*," he said, closing his phrase book. "Please tell Mr Fin Tan that's the message from young Fintan, OK?"

The man's shocked expression suggested it wasn't OK at all. Whatever Fintan had said it probably wasn't what he meant to say! The Scarlet Whirlwind let out a sudden outraged shout and began scaling the wall of the temple. Fintan was amazed at how quickly and easily he moved. It was like watching a large angry cat in red pyjamas. Within seconds the man had bounded up all five of the curving roofs and was heading right at him.

"I could get him something else, if you like?" suggested Fintan, realizing he might actually be in danger.

The Scarlet Whirlwind wasn't listening. He launched himself into the air, did a double somersault and landed squarely on his feet next to Fintan. With lightning speed he began swishing his arms around in a complicated kung fu sort of way. His red silk sleeves flapped noisily. Then, with a blood-curdling shriek, he leapt at Fintan, missed and fell off the balcony.

It had all happened a bit too fast to see but he appeared to have trodden on Fintan's greasy pork sandwich. An oily gravy skid mark was all that remained of it. Fintan watched wide-eyed as the man tumbled down the many roofs in a hail of broken terracotta tiles.

THIRTY-TWO

Inside the temple, Gribley was still studying the mural of the dragon. It was definitely the same shape as the river but where exactly along it was the lost village? There was no 'X' marking the spot and the Black River was hundreds of kilometres long! Something must be missing.

He paced around the ancient stone floor, deep in thought. Despite its great age the floor was in excellent condition. All apart from one small area beneath the dragon where there was a shallow dent.

He was just bending down to investigate when his concentration was interrupted by a series of loud thumps from above. The whole ceiling shook and a shower of dust drifted down. Amazingly the falling dust neatly filled the dent in the floor.

Gribley stared up in disbelief. A narrow shaft of sunlight was flooding in through a small hole in the ceiling. It marked an exact point at a sharp bend in the dragon's body.

"The location of Yin!" he breathed, as the puzzle finally pieced itself together.

There really was an 'X' to mark the spot! The dent in the stone floor must have been caused by many years of rainwater dripping through the hole. At some point in time the monks must have repaired it, accidentally hiding the vital clue.

But why had it suddenly reapperared? What could have caused the ancient secret to reveal itself while he was standing there looking for it? It was an unbelievable stroke of luck!

As he gazed up again his questions were answered. Fintan's face appeared at the hole.

"Oh hello, Gribs." he said, "That wasn't me, honest."

THIRTY-THREE

Despite all the previous day's chaos, the monks allowed Fintan and Gribley to stay in the temple overnight. Apart from snoring like a boar with asthma, Fintan behaved himself quite well and slept even better; until dawn broke, anyway. For some bizarre reason monks got up at five o'clock in the morning and started chanting and ringing little bells.

"Couldn't they do that a bit later?" whined Fintan, pulling his sleeping bag over his head.

"It is their normal routine, sir," explained Gribley. "And it has been their normal routine for over a thousand years. We can't expect them to change it just because they have guests sleeping over."

After a simple but filling breakfast they thanked their hosts and set off on the last leg of their journey.

It began very well. Descending the mountain path was far easier than going up and the morning air in the forest was pleasantly cool. Just right for a day's walking.

Gribley was feeling unusually excited too. They were on their way to the lost village of Yin, where no one had set foot for eight hundred years, and they actually knew its location! Well, roughly. The lost village was somewhere near a sharp bend in the Black River and was probably hidden beneath centuries of foliage. The chances of there being much left of it were very slim indeed, but it was still a thrilling thought!

They headed west through the forest in good spirits. The terrain wasn't too difficult and the route was mostly downhill. Gradually the pine trees gave way to a different sort of habitat and they entered bamboo forest. Mile upon mile of impossibly tall bamboo trees swayed in the slight breeze, split by the occasional shaft of misty sunlight. It was stunning.

Suddenly Fintan, who had been trusted with the map and was leading the way, stopped and began poking at something on the ground.

"Panda poo!" he announced in an excited whisper. "They must be nearby!"

He picked up a few dry clumps of something that looked like little rugby balls made of breakfast cereal and sniffed them.

Gribley arched an eyebrow. "Really, sir?" he said, surprised that the boy now thought he was an expert on panda droppings.

"Smells like bamboo," said Fintan, proudly popping them into his pocket. "Brilliant!"

It wasn't as good as having an actual panda to take home but they would make a really good souvenir and unlike Stripy Steve they wouldn't run away.

There was a look of utter astonishment on Gribley's face. Normal people bought postcards and little ornaments as souvenirs, didn't they? Not unidentified animal droppings!

Just as they were about to set off again something moved in the undergrowth nearby. Fintan and Gribley both froze. There was a creature in there crunching and chomping at the leaves. It was hard to see through the tangle of bamboo but it looked like a large, hairy, black and white bear!

"Good grief!" whispered Gribley, hardly daring to believe it. "It's a giant panda, sir!"

Fintan beamed with delight and gave a thumbs-up gesture.

"I knew it!" he hissed.

As quietly as possible they edged forwards, crouching low to the ground trying not to scare it away. Amazingly the panda didn't mind being stared at. It just sat there and carried on eating. For the next five minutes Fintan and Gribley enjoyed the company of one of the rarest animals on earth in its natural habitat. It was wonderful.

It was only when Fintan tried to get a little closer that the panda seemed to notice them at all. This was probably because he dropped his rucksack and half the contents fell out. At first the panda looked a bit wary but it didn't run or, worse still, attack. After a while an inquisitive black nose poked through the bushes and began sniffing at the pile of scattered stuff on the ground. It seemed to be really interested in Fintan's sleeping bag, possibly because of the faint smell of peanut butter it was giving off. After a while it stood up, lumbered over to Fintan's belongings, and began sorting through them with a big hairy paw. It appeared to like them very much. Then it sat on them and went to sleep.

Three hours later Fintan and Gribley reached the edge of the bamboo forest. However, only one of these hours had been spent walking; the other two had been spent trying to get their things back from a bad-tempered panda.

"We appear to have reached the Black River, sir," announced Gribley as they stopped by a broad expanse of muddy water.

"Brilliant," said Fintan, dumping his backpack on the ground and taking a swig from his water bottle.

He stared along the fast-flowing river. It stretched way off into the distance, still shrouded in morning mist. "So what do we do now, Gribs?" he asked.

"We follow the river upstream, sir, until we reach the area which I highlighted on the map."

Fintan nodded. "OK. How far's that, do you think?"

"I'm afraid I can't say, sir," said Gribley, sounding a little irritated. "Because our map was eaten by a giant panda."

"I said I was sorry, Gribs!" insisted Fintan. "And be fair, it only ate *some* of the map."

"Indeed it did, sir. But it tore up the rest of it and used it as bedding."

Fintan frowned, feeling a bit hard done by. After all, it was *his* sleeping bag that was covered in panda slobber and *his* socks that had been chewed to a mushy pulp, not Gribley's!

After a short rest they set off again. The river led them on a long winding course which went on for mile after mile. They waded through swampy water, squidged through stinky mud and pushed through waist-high grass. But no matter how far they walked their surroundings looked exactly the same. The same fast-flowing brown water. The same deep valley, thick with trees. The same clouds of annoying little insects that followed them all the way.

"Any idea what we're looking for, Gribs?" asked Fintan. "I mean, I know it's the lost village of Yin but how will we know when we find it?"

"Again, sir, I'm afraid I don't know," sighed Gribley.

Without the map he couldn't even be sure where they were.

"Isn't there some sort of landmark we could look out for?" continued Fintan. "You know, like Horseshoe Bend or something? The famous landmark on the Colorado River?"

Gribley was impressed. Perhaps the boy knew something about geography after all!

"How do you know about that, sir?" he asked.

"Oh, there was a big thing in *Young Adventurer* magazine once," explained Fintan. "Famous landmarks on famous rivers, it was called."

"I see," said Gribley.

"There was also a picture of the Iguana Falls of Peru," continued Fintan, eager to show off his knowledge, ". . . and the Caves of Lugogo in Swaziland, and the Bowing Sisters in China, and the—"

Gribley stopped him in mid-sentence. "I beg your pardon, sir, but what did you just say?"

"The Bowing Sisters," said Fintan again "Wait . . . is that anywhere around here, then?"

There was a short stunned silence.

Fintan wondered why his butler suddenly looked so excited and was holding his forehead in both hands.

"It's a third clue!" exclaimed Gribley. "The Great Master left a third clue and it's been staring me right in the face!"

"Has it?" asked Fintan.

Gribley nodded excitedly. "I believe the Bowing Sisters are indeed somewhere around here, sir. They are the most famous landmark along the Black River, consisting of a pair of large rocks which resemble human figures bowing to each other. At the temple I was shown an image of two bowing women . . . carved by the Great Master. Why didn't I see the clue before?"

Fintan didn't know and shrugged to demonstrate the fact.

"The lost village of Yin must be near the Bowing Sisters! If we can find the Sisters we can find Yin!"

"Brilliant," said Fintan happily. "I told you *Young Adventurer* was good, didn't I!"

THIRTY-FOUR

Fin Tan felt dreadful. There were no cigarettes left at all, and there was nothing he could do about it. Even thumping poor Mr Pong wasn't making him feel any better. He had just started pacing back and forth when a sudden idea occurred to him. Why not send some of the power station workers out in search of cigarettes! There were plenty of them after all. Surely a few could be spared for such an important mission! He clumped back into the turbine hall and made an announcement.

"Listen, you men," he yelled, while handing out all the cash from his wallet. "This is an emergency. Go and buy me cigarettes. As many packets as you can, understand? I don't care where you have to go, but don't come back until you've got them!"

The men did as they were told, hurried outside and drove off in an assortment of old cars and trucks. Mr Pong picked himself up from the ground and went with them. He'd had quite enough of being punched.

Seconds later Fin Tan's phone rang and he snatched it up again.

"Tell me you've found cigarettes!" he demanded, a bit optimistically.

The men had only just left after all.

"Pardon?" said a croaky voice.

It was the Scarlet Whirlwind and he didn't sound very well. He had just fallen off a tall building and tumbled down a mountain after all. That sort of thing can leave a few bruises!

"Oh, it's you," snapped Fin Tan. "In that case, tell me you've captured the boy!"

"Er, well . . . not exactly, boss," said the Scarlet Whirlwind sadly. "I tracked him to the Temple of the Sky and I ordered him to come with me. But he attacked me, boss. I don't know how but somehow he pushed me off the roof!"

"He did what?" yelled Fin Tan, shuddering with rage. "The boy defeated YOU?"

What kind of person were they dealing with here? Some kind of super-skilled martial arts expert? Was the boy a miniature kung fu killing machine? One by one Fin Tan's mighty Knot of Blood had been wiped out by this irritating little foreign boy. Even the Scarlet Whirlwind himself had been beaten in unarmed combat and reduced to a gibbering wreck! It was intolerable!

"I am truly sorry, Mr Fin Tan, sir," continued the trembling voice. "But before he attacked me he sent you this message. He says that you have lost and that you will be thrown away. He says he is the new Fin Tan."

The fat man's face flushed dangerously red and wobbled like raspberry jelly.

"New Fin Tan?" he roared, hurling his phone against the wall. "Never! There can be only ONE Fin Tan!"

THIRTY-FIVE

"So, these Bowing Sisters. . ." said Fintan, straining his imagination. "Have they got like girls' faces and long hair and dresses and stuff?"

Gribley feared he may have confused the boy. "Not exactly, sir," he said. "Perhaps you should just look out for some large bent rocks, one on either side of the river."

Their conversation was interrupted by the sound of an engine approaching. There was a small fishing boat chugging up behind them and standing on it was the first human they had seen since leaving the temple: a very thin old woman dressed all in black, wearing one of those circular rice paddy hats. She had just landed a large wriggling fish and was busy hitting it with a stick.

"Look, Gribs, a boat!" said Fintan excitedly. "Let's see if we can get a lift!"

Gribley got out his phrase book and started looking for the appropriate words while Fintan started waving his arms about and shouting.

"Excuse me, miss," he yelled. "Can you give us a lift, please?"

The old woman ignored him and continued whacking her fish.

"We're looking for the lost village of Yin," added Fintan while pointing upstream.

It made no difference. She didn't appear to be stopping for them.

"Master Fintan, sir," interrupted Gribley. "I don't think she speaks any English."

It was true, she didn't. However, she had just heard someone shout the words "Fin Tan", which appeared to have struck fear into her old heart. She immediately cut the boat's noisy engine and steered it to the riverbank.

"Fin Tan?" she said nervously.

It was apparently a name you shouldn't ignore. All of a sudden she seemed very happy to give them a lift and ushered them on to her boat with a big nervous smile. She had three appallingly bad teeth. Fintan wondered whether she might be Mr Pong's mum.

"Pleased to meet you!" he said, climbing aboard and shaking her bony hand.

The boat was small and cramped and stank of fish but it was much better than walking the rest of the way. Once her passengers were safely onboard, the woman started up her noisy outboard motor again and continued upstream.

Gribley thumbed through his phrase book until he found the words for Bowing Sisters. He tried pronouncing it several different ways but the old woman just stared at him.

"Are you sure you're saying it right?" asked Fintan. "Let me have a go."

He tried his best, but it still didn't work. In the end they resorted to miming. Fintan and Gribley stood either side of the boat and pretended to be women bowing to each other.

"Ah, Bowing Sisters!" grinned the old woman, nodding her head. Perhaps she did speak a little bit of English, after all.

*

As the day wore on, the river grew steadily rougher and dirtier. Instead of trees lining the banks there were now chunks of rusting machinery, dumped and forgotten. Fintan was just wondering whether this was why it was called the Black River when the old woman stood up and pointed ahead.

"Bowing Sisters," she announced.

The boat rounded a bend in the river and, right in front of them, there they stood: a matching pair of big, bent rocks. As expected, they didn't look much like sisters at all, even if you screwed up your eyes and used your imagination. Unfortunately, stretched between the sisters was a massive, very ugly concrete dam.

"Oh dear," said Gribley.

Fintan was confused. "You never said anything about there being a huge great dam here, Gribs!" he said. "That would've been a *much* easier landmark to spot."

The old woman quickly pulled over to the bank. She seemed to be in a hurry to turn around and leave.

"Thank you for your kind help, madam," said Gribley, stepping on to the bank while Fintan missed it and stumbled into the muddy river.

Once the boat had gone, they stood and stared at the grim, industrial ugliness that lay before them. For Gribley it was an unbelievable disappointment. What sort of idiots would build a hydroelectric power station in such a beautiful and historical place? It was a disaster. Both sides of the river were a treeless stretch of scrubby wasteland covered in patches of oil and broken machinery. The burnt out remains of thousands of cigarettes lay trodden into the earth. Litter blew around in the wind and flapped from the bushes like nasty, little plastic flags.

"Is this Yin?" asked Fintan, sounding very confused. "I can't see why anyone would want to write poems about this place!"

"No, sir," explained Gribley sadly. "This is Mang Kee."

"It certainly is!" said Fintan, screwing up his nose and scraping something disgusting off his boot. "So shall we ask if anyone knows where Yin is?"

Gribley now feared there was probably nothing left of it at all but decided not to say anything; the boy would need to be let down gently.

They hoisted up their backpacks and walked

towards the dam. Fintan had never stood next to anything quite so enormous before. It was a towering wall of reinforced concrete topped with rusty iron cranes. At its foot, straddling the river, was Mang Kee power station: a large brick-shaped lump covered in electricity pylons and thousands of power lines. The main door wasn't locked so they let themselves in and clumped up a metal staircase. The air inside was humid and smelt of sweat and misery. It was also completely deserted.

Two storeys up they found themselves in a stunningly large, cavernous space. It was so enormous that they felt like a pair of flies sitting on the floor of a school hall. Fintan peered over a metal railing into a deep pit where rows of huge turbines were filling the air with a low throbbing noise. It was a confusion of pipes, control panels and gauges, but not a single person appeared to work there.

"Wonder where everyone is?" said Fintan, dumping his rucksack on the floor and wiping the sweat from his face.

"Indeed, sir," agreed Gribley. "Perhaps we should try upstairs?"

They took a lift up to the next level, which contained yet more machinery, but no people. Above that was an empty rest area littered with half-eaten meals at abandoned tables. The whole place was completely deserted. Fintan was just about to press the lift button again when the lift door slid open and a Chinese man dashed out. He was wearing a greasy boiler suit and an orange hard hat, and looked extremely distressed. The man stopped and grabbed Fintan by the shoulders.

"*Kung sha?*" he screeched in an urgent voice.

"Who?" said Fintan, assuming it was a case of mistaken identity. "No, this is Gribley and I'm Fintan. Neither of us is called Kung Sha. Sorry."

Gribley braced himself, he had never heard the phrase "*kung sha*" before but it sounded very serious. At first he thought they had been caught trespassing and were about to be thrown out. Or perhaps there was some sort of emergency happening. But wouldn't there be red flashing lights or blaring sirens? It seemed unlikely.

"*Kung sha?*" yelled the workman again, turning his attention to Gribley.

"Awfully sorry," he said, shaking his head.

"Don't suppose you know where Yin is, do you?" asked Fintan hopefully.

The man had no idea what he was saying and just looked desperate. After a few seconds of general confusion he gave up and ran off down the metal steps, presumably to look for Kung Sha somewhere else.

Undeterred, Fintan and Gribley took the lift up to the top floor. It was their last chance of finding anyone who might be able to help them. As the door opened, two more men in orange safety hats rushed in, and began grabbing at them in the same way.

"We're not Kung Sha!" announced Fintan before either of them had a chance to ask.

Once they had shaken the men off, they pushed their way out of the lift and into a large, well-furnished office. It was full of the usual things that rich bosses like to surround themselves with: expensive paintings, sleek lighting and, of course, an abnormally large desk with a swivelling leather chair. In pride of place on the far wall there was also a huge red, knotted tassel, about ten times the size of the one Fintan had. Weirder still, there was a big fat man in the middle of the room, strangling someone. Fintan and Gribley stopped still, wondering what on earth they had just walked in on. The fat man suddenly became aware that he had visitors and stared at them with his little piggy eyes.

"You!" he demanded, letting go of the unfortunate workman's throat. "You got *kung sha*? Have you got any cigarettes?"

"Ohh!" said Fintan.

So that was what *kung sha* meant!

"No, we haven't. We don't smoke, do we, Gribs?"

Gribley shook his head very slightly but said nothing. This enormous man looked a bit scary. The worker he had been strangling wiped the tears from his eyes, then staggered off to join his frightened colleagues. He was the last one to go. The entire Mang Kee power station workforce had now been sent out to buy their boss some cigarettes. Apart from the three people standing in the office, Mang Kee was completely deserted.

"Hello," said Fintan cheerily, putting on a big smile. "This is Gribley and I'm Fintan and we're looking for the lost village of Yin. It's meant to be somewhere around here so we were wondering if you might have seen it?"

For a moment the big fat Chinese villain just stood there breathing heavily and scrutinizing his uninvited visitors. He could hardly believe it, but his arch-enemy had just wandered into his secret hideout . . . voluntarily! It was a bit of a shock. Was this really the person who had wiped out the Knot of Blood? The person who had put Fang in hospital, and knocked the stuffing out of the Scarlet Whirlwind? But he was so small! Surely this skinny, little kid didn't think he could finish off the mighty Fin Tan, too! If so, the foolish boy was in for a very nasty surprise. Fin Tan lumbered right up to him, pointing to his own huge, sweaty chest.

"You are not Fin Tan," he growled. "I . . . am Fin Tan!"

"Really?" laughed Fintan, realizing what a bizarre coincidence it was. "Well, fancy that!"

Ten minutes later no one was laughing. Fintan and Gribley found themselves tied back to back and dangling over the edge of the dam. Neither of them had any idea why. They had been hoisted up on a crane and winched out into mid-air. Below them was nothing but a terrifyingly long drop into the huge, dark lake. It was just like a scene from a movie.

"So. . ." said the fat gangster, pacing back and forth on the top of the dam. "You thought you could get away with it, did you?"

A short silence followed, broken only by the creaking of the rope. Fintan racked his brain. Get away with what? It couldn't possibly be about the stacking doll, could it? If so it was a major overreaction. This Fin Tan bloke must be nuts!

"Are you still upset about your present?" he asked. "Because I haven't got it any more, honest, and it wasn't my fault anyway. I gave it to that Fang lady to give to you and she threw it—"

"Be quiet, boy!" snapped the fat man. "No talking . . . just dying!"

He looked very pleased with himself for thinking of this line. It was exactly the sort of thing that the big villains said in films. He threw back his head and laughed an evil laugh.

"Maybe now you will learn not to mess with Fin Tan?"

"OK," agreed Fintan, nodding his head. "I've definitely learnt my lesson. You can let us down now."

"Please," added a very confused Gribley.

Fin Tan ignored them and smiled nastily with his fat, toady lips. He had no intention of letting them go.

"Notice how the rope runs around the pulley," he continued, pointing to the arm of the crane swinging above their heads. "Also notice how the other end of the rope is attached to this clock mechanism. As the clock ticks, the pulley slowly lowers you down. All the way down to the bottom of the lake. A very unpleasant way to die, yes?"

Fintan and Gribley looked down and had to agree. It sounded very unpleasant indeed.

"Of course," continued Fin Tan casually, "I would like to stay and watch you die but I have important business to attend to. I bid you goodbye."

After a bit more chuckling at his own evil brilliance he waddled off, leaving Fintan and Gribley dangling helplessly in the air.

"Well that was weird!" snorted Fintan, as the fat man disappeared into the lift.

Gribley said nothing. He was struggling to reach the small emergency penknife he kept in his sock. The ropes were very thick and he didn't have much time to cut through them. Every few seconds the pulley jerked and dropped them a few centimetres closer to the water. Things were looking pretty bleak. Fintan, however, still seemed surprisingly relaxed.

"I wonder why they always do that, Gribs?" he said ponderously.

"I beg your pardon, sir?"

"These super-villain people. Why do they always invent these complicated ways of bumping people off? I mean, he could have just shot us or something, couldn't he? Why's he bothering to do all this stuff with cranes and pulleys and clocks and things? Who has stuff like that just lying around anyway?"

Gribley wasn't very familiar with this particular movie cliché. He tended not to watch action films.

"I'm afraid I don't know, sir," he said, still tugging at the ropes.

Fintan, however, had seen hundreds of action movies and couldn't believe how corny it all was.

"Come to think of it," he went on, warming to his

theme, "who makes their super-villain hideout in a hydroelectric dam? What's wrong with a house? And why did he just go away and leave us here without waiting to see if his plan worked? How does he know we won't escape? Super-villains are a bit dim, eh, Gribs?"

Gribley wasn't really listening.

"Indeed, sir," he agreed as the pulley clicked another turn downwards.

He couldn't bring himself to say it but he feared they weren't going to escape this time. Real life wasn't like the movies at all.

THIRTY-SIX

Fin Tan had really enjoyed bullying his prisoners but he had more important things on his mind. Like cigarettes! He was fidgety, crotchety and irritated. Beads of sweat were dripping down his big, chubby face and he couldn't stop clenching his podgy fists.

As he made his way through the turbine hall, he caught sight of Fintan's rucksack lying on the floor and swung a kick at it. It flew through the air, hit a wall and burst open. He stomped through the scattered contents, kicking them aside like a huge enraged child. However, amid all the grubby socks and underpants and half-eaten sandwiches, something caught his eye. It was a brightly coloured Russian stacking doll. Greedily he snatched it up and shook it. There was something rattling around inside that might just be a cigarette. He wrenched the top off but found just another smaller doll. He snarled with frustration and yanked that one open, too. Three dolls later he reached the smallest one. It was just big enough to hold one single cigarette. If he didn't find something to smoke soon he was going to explode! With a desperate gleam in his piggy little eyes he ripped it open. And exploded.

THIRTY-SEVEN

Fintan and Gribley were now up to their necks in the lake. Every few seconds the clock ticked and the rope lowered them a little deeper. Even Fintan was starting to think they might not survive.

"So . . . at least you got to see China, eh, Gribs?" he said, trying to sound cheerful. "Like you always wanted to. That was good, wasn't it?"

"Indeed it was, sir," said Gribley, raising his chin above the surface. "And may I say what a pleasure it was to accompany you on the expedition."

A small wave sloshed against Fintan's face, filling his mouth with water.

"Thanks, Gribley, old friend," he spluttered. "And it was a pleasure for m—"

His sentence was interrupted by something

powerful thumping against his legs. At first he thought it must be a shark, which was probably the only thing that could make their situation any worse. But it wasn't a shark. It was a shock wave; a deep rumbling vibration from somewhere below them that threw a surge of water right over their heads. The second they resurfaced the noise hit them. An unbelievably loud boom thundered through the air and echoed along the valley. Everything shook. Chunks of concrete split off from the dam and tumbled into the water all around them.

"What on earth was that?" yelled Fintan.

Gribley suspected it may have been an explosion. And also a miracle.

The water level was suddenly dropping fast and within seconds it was down to chest height. Fintan stared down as his soggy shorts and dangling legs were uncovered. It was like someone had pulled the plug out from a massive bath.

"Where's the lake going, Gribs?" he asked, spitting out a mouthful of water.

"I'm not entirely sure, sir," said Gribley. "But I do believe we're saved!"

Way below them Rottervich's bomb had blown a huge hole in the dam. Thousands of gallons of water were gushing into the turbine hall and smashing it apart. Power lines were being torn down, sparking and flashing. Pieces of machinery weighing many tons were being ripped up from the floor and thrown around like toys. Huge heavy turbines bashed against the concrete pillars that held up the dam, splitting and crumbling them. The noise was unbelievable; it sounded like an angry giant was smashing up a scrapyard with a hammer. Floor by floor the dam began to collapse. It folded in on itself sending Fin Tan's fabulous office and lavish living quarters tumbling into the devastation below. His priceless art collection and luxury furniture were mangled and crushed and his champagne-filled fountain would never be the same again.

In less than a minute the churning wave was storming on down the valley dragging a mess of debris with it. Among the wreckage was a huge portrait of Fin Tan broken in half and the ragged remains of a large red knotted tassel. There was no sign of Fin Tan at all.

On Fintan and Gribley's side of the dam, however,

things were looking up. The view was improving all the time. As the lake dropped lower and lower, the upper branches of a long-drowned forest became visible, blackened after many years underwater.

"Look, Gribs," said Fintan, pointing with one foot. "I can see trees!"

Gribley had finally managed to get the little penknife from his sock and was attempting to transfer it to his teeth to start working on the rope. With his arms pinned to his sides it wasn't an easy task.

"A most welcome sight indeed, sir," he grunted.

The knife was more suited to removing splinters and sharpening pencils. It was going to take a long time to cut through their bonds.

"And look at that, Gribs," continued Fintan excitedly. "It's an old funfair or something."

Gribley found this a little harder to believe.

"I beg your pardon, sir?" he mumbled with the knife between his teeth.

Fintan nodded his head towards a semicircle of rotten wood which had broken the surface. "Over there, look. That must've been the big wheel."

It certainly looked like one so it was an easy

mistake to make. Gribley's eyes widened as more of the structure was revealed. It was an ancient water wheel! Beneath it were stone pillars and beautifully built walls. Gradually the remains of red-tiled roofs and stone steps were exposed and even the shapes of narrow streets became clear. Everything was coated in a film of mud but in places the glint of gold was visible.

"Good grief . . . we've found it!" muttered an awestruck Gribley.

"Found what?" said Fintan.

"Yin!" breathed Gribley. "We've found Yin!"

It took the slowly ticking mechanism ten minutes to lower them all the way to the ground. Fintan and Gribley, who were now unbelievably excited, couldn't wait. Gradually the deafening roar of the flood died down and in the far distance they could hear the wailing of sirens. By the time they reached the bottom, the enormous lake had shrunk back to the river it had once been. Instead of a terrible death by drowning they found themselves dunked knee deep in muddy water. It was a miraculous escape.

"There!" announced Gribley as his little knife cut through the last strand of rope and released them both.

Fintan dropped a bit deeper into the soft mud of the riverbed. "Brilliant!" he said, struggling to stand upright. "Fancy hiding a knife in your boot! Genius! We can always rely on you, eh, Gribs?"

They waded out of the river. There, spread out before them, lay the long-lost village of Yin, waiting to be explored. It was overgrown by a tangle of long-dead trees but looked amazingly well preserved. It must have been swallowed by the forest long before disappearing beneath the lake. Most of the old stone houses were still standing exactly as they had been left hundreds of years before. Clay pots still stood by doorways and iron farm tools lay rusting where they had been abandoned. Beautiful little bridges arched over walkways and tall pagodas towered above them. It was an incredible sight. Unspoiled and unbelievable!

Together they explored the maze of old streets and alleyways, peering through windows into a forgotten world. Every single building they investigated, from large impressive dwellings to small storehouses, was filled with fascinating lost artifacts.

"This is absolutely wonderful!" breathed Gribley with an awestruck expression on his face. "To think that the Great Master himself walked these very streets all those years ago."

"Yep, eight hundred years ago," added Fintan, to show that he'd been paying attention. "And we're the first people to set foot here since!"

In places they could even see signs of the village's last days. The warlord's men had definitely attacked the place in their search for the Master. Walls were blackened and fire damaged and only held together by trees. But there was still evidence of the Great Master's work. Everywhere they looked they found spectacular carvings in his unmistakable style. All of them had been defaced. Some showed signs of being hacked at with axes and smashed with rocks. Others had been completely destroyed but it was still unmistakably the Great Master's work. And all of them completely unknown!

Scenes of everyday village life had been cut into walls and curved dragon bodies decorated stone monuments. Around the next corner was an even greater surprise. Beyond a decorative gateway stood a stunningly beautiful temple. Its curving roof was topped with a pair of golden dragons holding the curved crescent of a glowing moon between them.

Fintan and Gribley climbed the marble steps to the open doorway in awestruck silence. This was turning out to be even better than Gribley had dared to imagine! In pride of place in the centre of the temple was a statue of a man cast in bronze. It was completely intact.

"Is that him, Gribs?" asked Fintan excitedly. "Is that the poet bloke?"

Gribley carefully wiped away the thin layer of mud. "I'm afraid not, sir. It's . . ."

He paused, not quite believing what he was seeing. "It appears to be a statue of the warlord."

Fintan looked blank so Gribley thought he'd better remind him.

"The warlord, sir? The rather unpleasant person who was so angry about one of the Great Master's poems that he sent his army to kill him?"

"Oh him," said Fintan. "But . . . hang on. Why would they have a statue of him here? I thought no one liked him?"

Gribley didn't know. Perhaps the warlord's men had put up the statue? But why would they do that in a village they had just attacked and left deserted? It was a mystery.

Meanwhile, out on the river another mystery was just arriving. Floating along on its back was an extremely bent, portable plastic toilet. Judging by its battered state it must have been in the river for some time. It jolted to a halt amid a snarl of branches and debris. And then the door began to creak open. A shaky hand pushed it up like a vampire lifting the lid of a smelly coffin. Moments later a filthy face appeared and surveyed its surroundings with a murderous, one-eyed scowl. It was Boris Rottervich.

Spending three days trapped in a floating toilet covered in sewage isn't much fun. It's the sort of thing that can put a person in a bad mood. So it was no surprise that when Rottervich finally crawled out of the Portaloo he was seething with rage. He was also wincing with pain, gasping with thirst and dripping with muck. With no idea of where he had ended up he staggered ashore and found himself in a very old, very muddy village. There was no one around and everything looked unbelievably ancient. Where was he? What kind of weird, drowned world had he arrived in? Had he gone back in time somehow? It looked like something from the thirteenth century. Was the plastic Portaloo some kind of revolting time machine? Something very strange was going on.

After stumbling through the deserted streets for a while he heard voices. They were coming from a strikingly beautiful gold temple. With very little energy left he limped up the steps and through the doorway . . . and thought he saw Fintan Fedora. It didn't seem possible. He wiped a dollop of gunk from his good eye but he wasn't seeing things. The boy was still there. The very same annoying boy that had betrayed him, poisoned him, poked his eye out and probably knocked him in the river, too. He was standing right there looking at an old statue.

Gribley was the first to notice they were being stared at.

"I don't wish to alarm you, sir," he said, "but there's someone watching us. And I'm afraid they don't look very friendly."

Fintan turned to look. "Oh yeah," he said.

Sure enough, there was a grimy zombie thing standing in the doorway. It was caked from head to toe in a stinking crust of dirt. Unsurprisingly Fintan didn't recognize it as being Boris Rottervich.

"Wonder what it wants?"

Seconds later it became perfectly clear what the creature wanted. It bared its gold teeth, snarled like a wild animal and began lurching towards him.

"You!" it croaked. "I will kill you!"

Fintan stepped back. His attacker smelt like a sewer. Whatever it was covered with, it certainly wasn't mud. The reeking thing shambled right up to him and swung a weak punch, missing him by miles.

"I will k—"

The sudden exertion proved too much for Rottervich. His one good eye rolled back in his head. He blacked out, buckled at the knees and fell forwards into the statue, headbutting its legs. A loud metallic clonk echoed around the temple. It was partly the sound of the ancient bronze statue fracturing and partly the sound of Rottervich's skull doing the same. He hit the muddy marble floor face down and lay unconscious.

"What a weirdo!" exclaimed Fintan, wondering why so many strangers attacked him for no reason. "Where do they all keep coming from, eh, Gribs?"

Before Gribley had a chance to offer his opinion they were interrupted by a menacing creak. The statue was splitting apart. Fintan and Gribley stared helplessly as the figure of the warlord snapped at the ankles and toppled off its plinth. It landed on Rottervich's head with a clang, but he was already too far gone to notice.

Gribley was horrified. This remarkable, mysterious ancient statue had been standing there undamaged for eight hundred years. It had survived the rampages of an invading army, the strangling grip of a forest and centuries of immersion in deep water. Five minutes with Fintan and it was a wreck.

"Hey look, Gribs," announced the boy. "It's all hollow. No wonder it broke!"

He stepped forwards and had a peek inside. "Oh wow! There's something stuffed inside the base, look!"

Gribley's shock immediately turned to fascination. Just visible in the dark space below the statue's feet was a glint of gold.

"Shall I get it out, Gribs?"

"Actually, sir . . ." said Gribley, sounding a little alarmed, "may I do it, please?"

He hadn't come all this way just to watch Fintan breaking Yin's fabulous secrets.

Gribley turned on his torch and shone it into the hollow plinth. He looked astonished. Then very gently he reached both arms in and slowly extracted the hidden item.

"What is it?" asked an excited Fintan, craning his neck for a better view.

"It's treasure, sir!" said an elated Gribley.

It was an extremely beautiful figurine of the Moon Dragon holding a sword curved like a thin crescent moon. About a metre long from head to tail, it was cast in solid gold with rubies for eyes.

"Wow!" breathed Fintan.

It was perfect! It was exactly the kind of treasure he had always dreamed of finding. Unique, stunningly exotic and unbelievably valuable. Best of all, it was something he could take home and wave in the faces of his rotten brother and sister! If this didn't shut them up nothing would!

"What's that thing in its mouth?" he asked, intrigued.

The dragon's mouth was holding a very fragile roll of parchment. Gribley suspected he knew exactly what it was but couldn't bring himself to say it. Barely daring to breathe, he slid the ancient paper free, examined it closely and gasped. A colossal smile appeared on his face.

"Do you remember I told you about the poet's unfinished masterpiece, sir, *The Song of the Moon Dragon*?"

Fintan vaguely remembered hearing something about it and nodded his head.

"Well, this is the rest of it, sir! He finished it after all!"

THIRTY-EIGHT

The following day Fintan and Gribley headed home, this time on the same plane. Both of them were exhausted and still feeling a little stunned by it all. They had only enjoyed a few quiet moments to themselves with the statue before the police had arrived. Several van-loads of them had turned up and swarmed all over the place, photographing things, measuring things and putting things in little plastic bags. Some of them had come to investigate the enormous explosion that had sent a tidal wave hundreds of kilometres downstream. Others were there to arrest Fin Tan and were disappointed that he had disappeared. However, they were very happy to re-arrest a wanted Russian criminal who they found lying unconscious on the ground.

Much to Fintan's surprise, the filth-covered zombie thing had turned out to be Boris "Dead-Eye" Rottervich! The police had thrown buckets of water over his face and identified him straight away. They had congratulated Fintan and Gribley for capturing him then dragged the unconscious man away by his smelly ankles.

In the end everything had turned out pretty well. Rottervich was in jail, the entire Knot of Blood were in hospital and Fin Tan was in thousands of tiny pieces. Plus, of course, they had found exactly what they were looking for and were returning home triumphant! Not only had they found the lost village of Yin, but the golden Moon Dragon and the lost manuscript, too. It was almost unbelievable! They wouldn't be able to keep them for long, of course; things like that belonged in a museum. Fintan had been disappointed at first as he was planning to take the golden statue into school and show off a bit, but he had got used to the idea now. He was even hoping the museum might name a new wing after him. "The Fintan Fedora – World's Most Brilliant Explorer Wing" perhaps? Gribley was just glad to have been able to read the rest of his favourite book before it disappeared into a glass case.

Fintan didn't stop smiling all the way home, but there was still something puzzling him.

"Gribs," he said ponderously, as they walked up the driveway to Fedora Hall. "I still don't get why there was a statue of what's-his-name there, the warlord bloke. And why were the dragon and the parchment hidden inside it. What was that all about?"

Gribley had been giving this some thought. "A good question, sir. I believe it must have been the idea of the Great Master. Fearing his writing would be discovered he must have sculpted a statue of the warlord and hidden the manuscript inside. It was the only thing in the village he knew the warlord's men wouldn't destroy. Very clever, don't you think?"

"Very clever!" agreed Fintan, stepping through the front door.

"I'll tell you who's very clever!" called his mother's thrilled voice from the landing. "My very clever little explorer, that's who!"

She came rushing down the stairs in an excited

flutter, gave him a big hug and made sure he took his dirty boots off.

"*So* glad you're back safely, dear," she went on. "Now, do come along into the lounge. I'm sure everyone can't wait to hear all about it!"

The whole family was there. Mr Fedora was sitting in his favourite chair reading *Cake Maker Monthly* magazine while Felicity and Flavian were perched on the sofa like hungry vultures waiting for a dead wildebeest to be brought in. They could hardly wait to hear what had gone wrong and make fun of their little brother again. As soon as they saw him they jumped up and crowded around, poking and grabbing at him.

"Look, loser boy's here at last!" screeched Felicity at the top of her voice. "Thought you'd got lost again!"

Flavian guffawed. "Oh my God, you actually made it back! So what happened this time? Usual disaster, I suppose?"

"Did you enjoy the cakes?" added Felicity with a big wink.

Both of them snorted with laughter.

"Now now, you two," chided Mrs Fedora. "Don't

be mean to your little brother."

Fintan ignored them both.

"Hello, Dad," he said, pulling a couple of things out of his jacket pocket.

Mr Fedora put down his magazine and shook the boy's hand. "Ah, welcome home, son."

"I got you this," said Fintan, handing his mother a novelty clockwork cat that waved its paw. He had bought it at the airport on the way home. It was nowhere near as nice as the Russian stacking doll but since he had lost his rucksack and everything in it, the tacky souvenir would have to do.

"It's not very exciting, sorry."

Luckily his mother was very good at pretending to like her present. She gave him a big kiss while making sure he stayed on the sheets of newspaper she'd put down to protect the carpet.

"Actually I did get you something better . . ." continued Fintan, "but I lost it."

"Ha! How typical!" snorted Felicity. "Baby brother would lose his brain if it wasn't stuck inside his head!"

"Yeah, but look at him, sis," giggled Flavian. "I reckon he lost his brain years ago!"

The pair of them dissolved into fits of laughter and high-fived each other.

"These are for you, Dad," said Fintan, still trying to ignore his annoying siblings.

It was a pair of bright red chopsticks with CHINA written on them.

"Very nice," said Mr Fedora, trying hard to look pleased. "So . . . how did it all go? Did you find what you were looking for?"

"Oh yes!" announced Fintan, smiling proudly. "In fact we found more than we were looking for, didn't we, Gribs!"

This was Gribley's cue to open his bag and reveal the golden dragon and the fragile manuscript. He placed them both on the coffee table for the family to admire. They all looked completely stunned. Flavian and Felicity's jaws actually fell open! By the time Gribley had finished explaining the story of the Great Master and the lost village, the family looked even more stunned.

"I say, well done, Gribley, old man!" said a hugely impressed Mr Fedora. "Are these things valuable, do you suppose?"

Gribley smiled. "Priceless, sir." he said.

The strained looks on Flavian and Felicity's faces suggested they were in genuine pain. How were they supposed to tease their little brother now?

"Er, yeah . . . good job, Gribley," muttered Flavian. "But I bet it was no thanks to the idiot boy!"

Felicity decided to join in. She couldn't stand the thought of Fintan getting any credit.

"Yeah," she sneered. "He probably just got in the way, right?"

"Not at all," corrected Gribley, sounding genuinely annoyed. "In fact I would say the success of our expedition was mostly due to your younger brother. Despite all evidence to the contrary, he refused to believe the search for Yin was pointless. He pressed on when others would have abandoned hope. It was his optimism and determination that led us to the Moon Dragon. In fact, the two of you should be really proud of him."

Felicity and Flavian looked as if they'd been slapped across the face. They gritted their teeth and fumed silently. Fintan was overjoyed. It was one of the happiest moments of his life!

"So . . . bath time for you, young man!" announced Mrs Fedora, who was more concerned by the grubby state of Fintan's face and hands. "Off you go and get cleaned up. Even intrepid explorers have to have their bath, don't they!"

Normal life had returned already. Fintan was halfway up the stairs when he heard his horrible brother and sister running up behind him.

"Oy, not so fast, loser boy!" snapped Felicity, holding out her hand expectantly. "Where's my present then?"

"Yeah!" added Flavian, poking him in the ribs. "We wanted presents too, remember? What did you get us?"

Fintan hadn't got them anything. Deliberately. He sighed and felt around in his jacket pockets to see if he had anything that might pass as a gift. There was nothing but congealed mud, a damp fortune cookie and a small plastic tub he'd forgotten about. He pulled it out and peeled off the top.

"Well . . . I know you like fancy foreign food," he said. "So I got you this."

He handed each of them a couple of small, dry,

grassy lumps shaped like rugby balls.

"Try it," continued Fintan. "It's a delicious Chinese delicacy . . . called Pan Da Dung."

Clive Goddard has been on plenty of disastrous adventures. He was once stranded in the USA by a volcanic eruption, has been chased by an angry ostrich in Swaziland, and had his rucksack soaked by a leaky toilet in Holland. He got sunburn in Hawaii, heatstroke in Namibia, a poisonous spider bite in South Africa and food poisoning in Thailand. He lost his camera in Tasmania, lost himself in Japan and got robbed in China (twice).

Clive Goddard didn't know he was a writer until this book happened. He thought he was a cartoonist. It was probably illustrating a dozen or so *Horribly Famous* books that gave him this idea.

When not travelling, drawing or writing, Clive lives in Oxford where he rides a bike, plays badminton and practices sleeping for long periods of time.

HAVE YOU READ FINTAN'S FIRST ADVENTURE?

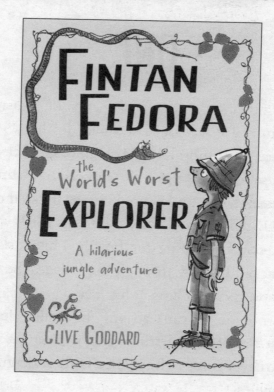

TURN OVER FOR A SNEAK PEEK...

ONE

The heat was unbearable. The air was thick with a thousand irritating little insects, crawling in Fintan's ears and up his nose. Sweat trickled down his back and legs and soaked into his thick woolly jungle socks. Gasping for breath, Fintan slashed and hacked his way through the foliage, the spiky exotic plants scratching at his face.

"It's no good, I can't go on!" he wailed, leaning against a mossy tree trunk and wiping his brow. "We're never going to find it in all this undergrowth. It's hopeless!"

"I fear you may be right, sir," came the calm, sensible voice of Gribley. "Perhaps it would be simpler just to buy another cricket ball."

Fintan took off his wide-brimmed hat and fanned

himself with it.

"I suppose so, Gribley," he sighed, "but it does mean our game has come to a sudden end . . . and it was my turn to bat, too!"

He was just hauling himself out of the undergrowth and back on to the beautifully kept lawn when his mother caught sight of him from the drawing room window.

"Fintan!" she shouted, with a voice that could crack mirrors and frighten dogs at a hundred paces. "What on earth do you think you're doing in my shrubbery? Kindly stop trampling all over my rhododendrons with your silly great boots!"

Fintan made a miffed sort of face, thrust his hands into his trouser pockets and kicked idly at a small prickly branch which had attached itself to his sock.

"Your father wants a word with you, by the way," concluded his mother, closing the drawing room window and returning her attention to her cacti collection. His father wanted a word? This wasn't something that happened very often. In fact, apart from the odd grunted "good morning" from behind his newspaper at the breakfast table, his father rarely spoke to him at all! Fintan wondered what he might have done wrong. Surely demolishing a rhododendron bush or two with a cricket bat wasn't serious enough to deserve a severe talking-to? This didn't sound good.

Fintan's older sister, Felicity, and his older brother, Flavian, were lounging in deck chairs on the lawn. There was nothing they enjoyed more than making fun of their accident-prone little brother and this was a perfect opportunity to do so.

"Oh dear! Looks like the idiot boy's in trouble again!" mocked Felicity loudly. "I wonder what he's broken this time?"

Flavian snorted with laughter and spilled a little of his drink. "Been naughty again, has he? Made his daddy cross?"

The pair of them laughed so hard at this thought that they had to wipe tears from their eyes and lemonade came out of their noses. Fintan ignored them as best he could. He'd been trying to ignore them for years.

Gribley coughed politely. "Perhaps you should go and see what your father wants, sir," he suggested. "And it would be wise to wash your face and hands first. I will see to it that the cricket equipment is cleared away."

After a quick splash in the wash basin, a slightly less grass-stained Fintan knocked on his father's study door.

"Come in," called a stern voice from within. Fintan pulled hard on the door handle, but it failed to open. He gave it a good hard tug, followed by a series of short rattling tugs, none of which achieved anything apart from making a lot of annoying noise.

"Push, you idiot!" said his father, sounding exasperated already. Fintan pushed with unnecessary force. He stumbled into the room like a drunk on roller skates, tripped over the rug and fell head first into a bookcase.

"Sorry, Dad!" he said, struggling to his feet and picking up some of the books from the floor. "I can never remember whether it's 'push' or 'pull' and—"

"Yes, yes, yes," interrupted his father, who had heard enough already. "Sit down, boy, I need to talk to you."

Fintan's father, Sir Filbert Fedora, was a formidable character. He was a large, old-fashioned-looking man with a ruddy face and a grey moustache the size of a fat squirrel. He had made his fortune in cakes. To be precise, he was the founder and chief executive of The Fedora Fancy Food Company – Purveyors of Fine Cakes and Biscuits. A huge portrait of him proudly holding a grand lemon tart assortment hung on the mahogany panelled wall behind him. Fintan sat in the squeaky red leather chair he was offered and peered nervously at his father across the enormous desk. Sir Filbert coughed into his hand, preparing to say something a little awkward.

"As you know, I'm not as young as I used to be. . ."

"Well, obviously you're not, Father! No one gets younger, do they! That would be impossi—"

"Will you please not interrupt me!" snapped his father. "Just listen! I'm getting to the age now where I'm considering retirement. Running The Fedora Fancy Food Company is too much work at my age, which is why I need to have this little chat with you. . ."

Fintan's eyebrows leapt up. He knew where this was leading. "No need to worry, Father!" he announced confidently. "The business will be safe in my hands. You can trust me!"

Sir Filbert coughed again, stood up and began

to pace around the room with his hands clasped behind his back.

"I'm afraid you misunderstand me, Fintan ... the problem is that we can't trust you."

Fintan's face fell and was replaced with a look similar to that of a small puppy who had just been told off for weeing on the carpet.

"I'm sorry, son, it's just that your mother and I have been talking and we think once you finish school, your talents would be better suited to ... er ... well ... to other areas. Leisure interests, for instance. I'm sure your brother and sister can manage the business perfectly well without you."

This last bit of news came as no surprise to Fintan. His goody-goody siblings, Felicity and Flavian, could do no wrong! They'd always been more popular, more successful and, well ... more everything! This was terrible! It wasn't fair! It was unjust!

"But you *can* trust me!" he protested. "I'd be really good at running the business!"

His father stopped pacing and looked sternly at him. "Really?" he said, staring straight into Fintan's puppy-dog eyes. "We can trust you, can we? What about the time we got you that hamster?"

"That wasn't my fault!" pleaded Fintan. "It got in the vacuum cleaner all on its own!"

"Maybe so, but you didn't have to try and get it out by turning the machine to blow! The mess took nearly a week to clean up! And what about the time we trusted you to organize that barbecue? Your mother was furious when those three fire engines turned up! They ruined the lawn!"

Fintan pulled a hurt face. "That wasn't my fault either! How was I to know that red bucket had petrol in it?"

Sir Filbert raised a hand, as if to say there was no point in arguing about it. "That's enough!" he said. "I'm afraid I've made my decision. Sorry, son. You'll just have to find something else to do with your future."

Fintan returned to his room, sat miserably on his bed and fumed. He'd show his father he wasn't useless!